WHEN IT RAINS

MARK ALLAN GUNNELLS

Crystal Lake Publishing
www.CrystalLakePub.com

Join the Crystal Lake community today
on our newsletter and Patreon!

ISBN: 978-1-957133-03-4

Cover art:
Ben Baldwin—http://www.benbaldwin.co.uk

Layout:
Lori Michelle—www.theauthorsalley.com

Proofread by:
Paula Limbaugh

WELCOME

TO ANOTHER

CRYSTAL LAKE PUBLISHING
CREATION

Excerpt from *The Day the Rains Came: An Annotated Timeline of the Deluge*

THE FORECAST FOR Greenville, SC, on April 24th, 20—, was clear and sunny with a high of 77 and a low of 54. The predicted chance of precipitation was zero percent. Allow me to repeat for emphasis: *zero percent.* In the years following what has commonly come to be known as 'The Deluge', meteorologists and other scientists have studied the phenomenon from all aspects. While there is still much that no one understands, many questions that remain unanswered, and countless conflicting conclusions, on one thing all the experts agree.

It should not have rained that day in Greenville, SC.

This is important to note because it shows that right from the onset, there was nothing natural about the Deluge.

The date in question did start off as expected. Sunrise was at 5:45am, and the day dawned as clear as promised. Not a cloud in the sky, and the air was warm with low humidity. When interviewed for this book, Eugene McArthur (a lifelong resident of Greenville, SC) described the day as "one of those perfect southern days made for picnics and long strolls." And yet at nearly 12:30pm, that perfect day would turn into a nightmare. The first stage of what would become a global disaster. The residents of Greenville, SC (population just over 58000 at the time), had no way of knowing that their quaint city was about to become the epicenter of an event that would change history.

11:35am

PAMELA WESTON HATED nice days.

"Grande Caramel Frappuccino," she announced, then handed the drink to a young blonde girl who snatched the cup and marched off.

Pamela turned back to the line that stretched all the way to the convenience section.

The young man next in line said, "I'd like a blueberry scone and a tall Iced Pineapple Matcha."

Shit! Not a drink with which she was familiar. She'd have to pull out the directions and fumble through it step by step, which would slow down the process even more. She grabbed the two-way radio by the register and said, "Jessica, I'm going to need you to come help me in the café."

A few seconds passed, then came the staticky reply: *"I'm kind of in the middle of something."*

Pamela groaned internally as three more students joined the line. "It can wait. Get up here *now*. Please."

She turned away from the waiting crowd, sure she could feel their annoyed stares drilling into her back, and began riffling through the book of drink recipes, looking for the Iced Pineapple Matcha.

When Pamela had taken the job as manager of the bookstore at Friedkin University two years ago, she'd thought it was a smart move. She'd been working at the Spartanburg County Public Library, a thankless job that mostly consisted of shooing out the homeless, and having her crotchety old boss tell her on a near-daily basis that she was too 'flighty' to ever be taken seriously in a professional setting. So when the campus bookstore position presented itself, she'd jumped at it, viewing it not only as a great opportunity but as vindication, proving that she was in fact managerial material.

And in all fairness, she had loved the job for the first year and a half. Sure, the weeks around new semesters were a crazy rush and annual inventory could be a headache, but the environment was so much more peaceful than the library, and her staff seemed to respect her. She, in turn, tried to always treat them with respect and understanding, never wanting to be like her previous supervisor. Of course, sometimes she felt she erred too far on the side of understanding, to the point that some of her employees saw her as a pushover. But 'rather too soft than too hard', as her grandmother used to say.

As she studied the instructions for the pineapple drink, out of the corner of her eye she noticed a few students leaving the line, grumbling and shooting Pamela nasty looks. Part of her saw these defectors as lost revenue for the store, but another part of her felt only gratitude and wished more customers would find the wait too long and give up. She glanced toward the back of the store, seeing no sign of Jessica.

"Jess, where are you?" she said into the radio.

"I just need to finish this one order."

"I said that could wait," Pamela answered, allowing a hard edge to creep into her voice. "I'm all alone up here, and I'm swamped."

She hoped that some of the customers, overhearing this conversation, would take a little pity on her—but their expressions suggested otherwise. She turned away from them again and started trying to put together the complicated drink.

For perhaps the millionth time in the past six months, she found herself cursing Angie, the previous café manager. Pamela realized this wasn't entirely fair. Angie had a right to take another position, and she'd worked out a full notice. It wasn't the young woman's fault that corporate had decided to hold off on filling the position, stating that Pamela could do double-duty for a while, managing both the bookstore and the café. No increase in pay came with these new responsibilities—but the headaches had increased threefold. Especially on nice days. Good weather brought more visitors onto campus. They walked around the lake right outside the bookstore, bringing in more business, particularly to the café side. Good weather also meant the café staff, made up mostly of students, were more likely to call out. Funny how these young people always seemed to get sick on warm, sunny days.

Today both the baristas scheduled for the morning had called out, Tanya claiming she had a stomach bug and Rudolph saying his grandmother was in the hospital. Pamela never used to be a cynical person, but she found herself having serious doubts about these stories. Yet in the end she'd simply wished them both well and realized she'd have to work the café alone.

Pamela overfilled the cup, spilling green liquid over her hand and the counter. Whispering an expletive, she snapped a lid onto the cup, wiped it down, then grabbed a scone from the bake case, throwing it on a plate.

The young man stared down at the scone and started, "Could I get that heat—"

When he glanced up at Pamela, he stopped mid-sentence and took his items. "Never mind. It's fine."

Finally Jessica came scuttling up from the back, taking her sweet time. When she'd made her way behind the counter, Pamela said, "Okay, I'm going to take orders. You make the drinks and—"

"Dr. Acker has requested a book for one of his summer classes. It's out of print and almost impossible to get. I tried explaining that to him, but he insists he needs that particular text. Nothing else will do. I've found a half dozen used copies through Textnet, but I need about a dozen more. I don't know what these professors expect—"

"Pause!" Pamela said. This was a technique she'd developed to halt Jessica's frequent rants. Though Jessica was at least twenty years Pamela's senior, at times Pamela felt like a parent trying to wrangle a hyperactive child. "We can discuss this later after Charlie comes in at two and can take over things here at the café. In the meantime, I'll take the orders, you make the drinks. Got it?"

Jessica looked unhappy, but then she always looked unhappy. Sometimes she reminded Pamela of that old cartoon dog that seems perpetually depressed even when he's happy. However, Jessica nodded her assent.

As Pamela took the next order, she found herself hoping desperately that Charlie wouldn't call out. He was her most reliable barista, but today had already turned into such a cluster, she wouldn't have been surprised by anything.

God, I hate nice days, she thought. *Why couldn't it be raining?*

11:50am

Eugene McArthur and his wife Helen wandered off the paved path that wound around Friedkin Lake, taking a seat in the wooden gazebo and watching a gaggle of geese float across the sparkling water in a V formation. Eugene took his wife's hand and squeezed it.

"Thanks for insisting we get out," she said, smiling at him. "It's too lovely to spend another day cooped up."

Eugene lifted Helen's hand and kissed the tips of her fingers. They had been married fifty-five years this past January, but she was still his best friend. The passionate side of their relationship had died down a long time ago, but what remained was companionship and a bond closer than biological family.

"I thought a little sunshine and exercise might do you good," he said. "But if you get tired, say the word and we'll head back to the car."

"Thanks, but I think I can make it the rest of the way around the lake."

They were on the far side from the parking lot next to the campus bookstore, and if they continued it would take them down past the clock tower before rounding back toward the dining hall and student center. Eugene had wanted to get Helen out into the world, but he worried about her overdoing it. Still, she seemed to have more energy today than she'd had in quite a while.

"This is a beautiful campus," Eugene said, staring off toward the outline of Paris Mountain.

"Mmm, it really is. Maybe on our way back around, we can stop at the rose garden."

"I don't know, maybe we should save that for another time."

Helen looked at him, her gaze steady and calm, her words firm and without self-pity. "There may not be another time, dear. I think we both know that."

Eugene felt tears prickling at the corners of his eyes, but he held them back. Helen was the one facing death, and yet she seemed so much stronger than him. She'd beat the cancer once, been in remission for over two years, but this time the doctors didn't hold out much hope. She had good days and bad, but the good were becoming fewer and farther between. In the silence of the home they had shared for over half a century, the sound of a ticking clock was loud and undeniable.

"Let's not dwell on the maudlin," she said, patting Eugene on the knee. "I don't want to waste the day. Let's keep going, and then maybe grab some sandwiches at the café. I'm feeling a little peckish."

Helen must have been feeling better, Eugene thought, because she hadn't had much of an appetite as of late. Pushing himself to his feet, ignoring the aches and pains of age, he helped his wife up. Holding hands, they started back toward the path.

11:55am

Tony Christensen had just finished taping up the box and was applying the address label to it when Yolanda stepped into the back area of the bookstore and said, "The café is really swamped. I feel sorry for Pamela and Jessica."

"I do too, but I can't really help them. They haven't trained me in the café yet."

"I hope Charlie doesn't call out, or I don't know what'll happen."

Tony shrugged. He felt bad about the situation, but there wasn't much he could do. He had started work as shipping/receiving supervisor only three weeks ago, and he was still learning how to do his own job. The café was another world entirely, and if he were to try to help, it would probably only slow matters down even more.

Stepping further into the back room, Yolanda picked up a maroon cap with the university's initials on the front. "I still can't believe people walk around with 'FU' on their clothes. Seems a bit tacky and crude to me."

"I thought your generation liked tacky and crude," Tony said.

"Don't judge us all by Cardi B."

Tony laughed, but truth be told he wasn't entirely sure who Cardi B was. He'd heard the name and surmised she was some sort of singer, but he didn't know much of anything about modern music. At forty-two, he never thought of himself as old, but now that he was surrounded by all these college students who weren't even born when *Friends* went off the air, he realized just how out of touch he was. Carlos, one of the other booksellers, had asked Tony once who his favorite singer was. When Tony answered with Melissa Etheridge, Carlos merely shook his head and said he'd never heard of her.

Feeling the vibration against his thigh, Tony reached into his pocket to retrieve his cell, reading the text.

"Your hubby?" Yolanda asked.

"Yeah, he's coming by around twelve-thirty to have lunch with me."

A bell *dinged* from out front and Yolanda said, "Customer, gotta jet." She left, then popped her head back through the doorway. "Make sure to introduce your husband to me when he gets here. I'd love to meet him."

Tony swaddled a coffee mug in bubble wrap and took a moment to muse on how much the world had changed just in his own lifetime. In his teens, he would never have imagined that he'd live to see the day when he would be able to legally marry the man he loved, much less be surrounded by people who treated that marriage with such casual acceptance. And here in the buckle of the Bible Belt, no less.

He took his phone out again and reread Vincent's text. Just a simple: *See you at 1230 <3*

Tony quickly texted back, *I don't say it enough but I love you.*

Two years married, five years together, and Tony still got excited about the prospect of a date with Vincent, even if it was nothing more than a quick twenty-minute lunch during a busy shift.

~

12:10pm

Dena Weathers had fallen in love with Friedkin University. She'd already been sort of in love with it, at least in deep *like*, from what she'd read online and the pictures she'd seen—but being here on the campus itself sealed the deal. Courtship was done, she was ready to make the commitment.

"This is the only school I want to go to," she told her parents as they walked down the steps from the library.

"Let's not get ahead of ourselves," her dad said.

"I've been accepted, what's the big deal?"

"You were also accepted by the University of South Carolina and Limestone College, both of which are a hell of a lot cheaper than this place."

"You get what you pay for," Dena said, turning one of her dad's favorite phrases back around on him.

Her mother laughed. "She's got you there, Jerry."

"Be that as it may, do you realize how much student loan debt you'll incur after four years here? It'll take a lifetime to pay off. I know people your age don't always cast a critical eye down the road, but a college education should enhance your future, not leave you financially crippled."

"You're so melodramatic," Dena said with a roll of her eyes. "Friedkin has the best curriculum of the three colleges I've gotten into, and the deadline to confirm with them that I will be attending in the fall is only a week away."

"I know," her dad said, "but I want you to make an informed decision; consider all the factors."

"Look, it's my college experience, right? Shouldn't I get to spend the next four years at the school I really want to go to?"

"She has a point, dear," her mother said.

Dena could always count on her mother to be on her side.

Her dad smiled. "I see I'm being outnumbered again. Fine, we'll sit down this evening and hammer out all the details."

Dena squealed and kissed her dad on the cheek. She'd initially been disappointed when she realized an out-of-state college was impractical and she'd need to find a local school to which she could commute, but Friedkin was everything she'd ever hoped for and more. She'd never realized such a gem was so close to home.

She wished she had been able to visit the campus earlier, but her dad's heart attack the week before Christmas had thrown all their lives into a tailspin. He was doing much better now, thank God, and though late in the game they were finally getting to visit the campuses before she made her final decision.

Since she was out for Spring Break this week, they'd started making the rounds. First they went to USC in Columbia. Seemed nice enough, but kind of grungy and nondescript. Limestone, which they visited next, had some beautiful buildings but the campus was tiny. Her mother had said it seemed the size of a postage stamp. Still, she had been leaning toward Limestone until they'd come to Friedkin this morning.

"Let's run back by the bookstore before we leave," she said.

"Why?" her dad asked.

"I want to get a Friedkin hoodie or sweatshirt. I mean, now that I've decided, I want to get some swag to wear to school next week."

"Already they're getting your money," her dad said, but he turned and started back toward the bookstore and the lake.

Her parents walked in front, and Dena practically floated behind them. She couldn't remember being so happy. Her high school experience hadn't been bad. She wasn't part of the most popular crowd, but neither was she one of the outcasts or geeks. She'd had a good group of friends, was Student Council Treasurer, and part of the choral club. And yet high school felt sort of empty to her. Maybe empty wasn't exactly the right word. More . . . frivolous. Like nothing that happened there really mattered, it was merely a training ground for the important stuff that would happen in college.

And she was finally about to enter that world. Even though she wouldn't be living on campus, she had no doubt Friedkin would begin to feel like a second home. Actually, she felt at home here already.

Up ahead, her mother stopped and stared off in the distance, using a hand to shield her eyes. "Wow, looks like the weather is about make a big shift."

Dena followed her mother's gaze and saw what she meant. Out over Paris Mountain, dark thunderheads had gathered like soiled cotton, lightning flashing within them. The clouds looked ominous and dangerous, the kind that would be hanging over a haunted castle in some old horror movie.

And they were moving fast, headed straight toward campus.

~~~

12:20pm

Vincent Phelps drove through the main gate of Friedkin University, wheeling around the traffic circle and taking the third turnoff. He glanced in the rearview mirror but quickly looked away, unable to meet his own eyes. He wished he'd at least had time for a quick shower before leaving Raul's, but that would have made him late for the lunch date with his husband and he didn't want to do anything that might arouse Tony's suspicion.

God, I'm a piece of shit. And a cliché one at that. Cheating on my husband like some common lowlife. Is this why I fought all those many years for marriage equality? Just for the chance to be an adulterer like all those slimy straight guys out there?

As usual when the guilt started to eat away at him, his mind tried to compensate with justifications and rationalizations. Although that was getting harder and harder to do these days.

He'd been faithful to Tony up until last year, when innocent flirtation with one of the security guards at work had led to a quick blowjob in the supply closet. He'd sworn to himself it was a one-time thing, but like a recovering alcoholic that gets pushed right off the wagon by a single sip of beer, before Vincent knew it he was trolling hook-up internet sites.

He kept telling himself it was only sex, nothing emotional, no actual feelings attached, and he convinced himself that made it better somehow.

And then he'd met Raul. What was meant to be a
~~~

one-night stand became a recurring thing. At first it had only been the sex that kept Vincent going back—intense and passionate and wild, whereas his love life with Tony had become routine.

Only after a while, he and Raul started talking after sex, getting to know one another, their trysts began leading to something more. Something closer to an actual relationship. Today Raul had said those three small but profound words: "I love you." Not only had Vincent said them back, but he'd meant them.

But he still loved Tony as well. He'd gotten himself into quite the predicament and had no idea how to get himself out again. No matter what, someone was going to get hurt.

Vincent didn't like to think of himself as a bad person, but going straight to meet Tony when he could still smell Raul on himself . . . well, he was out of excuses. He was a piece of shit, simple as that.

The day, previously sunny and bright, had turned cloudy and overcast, almost as if Mother Nature herself were casting judgement on him. In fact, as he turned right at the gymnasium to make his way to the bookstore, the first of the rain splattered against his windshield.

Excerpt from *The Day the Rains Came: An Annotated Timeline of the Deluge*

12:23:15PM. That has been determined to be the precise time the rain began to fall in Greenville, SC. Why of all the places in the world did the phenomenon start in this mid-sized southern town in the United States? That remains one of the myriad mysteries surrounding the Deluge. However, within a span of half an hour, the rain would spread across the entire globe.

Raining in every corner of the earth at the same time. That would have been unprecedented enough, but the strange and inexplicable nature of the rain made it more than a mere curious anomaly. It made the phenomenon one of the great mysteries of the universe.

Of course, at first no one in Greenville realized what effects the rain would have on those that came into direct contact with it. Initially, what struck people was the rain's unusual consistency.

12:23pm

EUGENE AND HELEN had just stepped through the side entrance into the café when the rain started. Not much at first, just a sprinkling of drizzle, as if God hadn't completely turned off the water in his shower and it dribbled from the head.

"In the nick of time," Eugene said with a chuckle.

"We still have to get back to the car."

Eugene eyed the long line and the two women scrambling to keep up with orders behind the counter. "Seems like we'll be here a while. Hopefully by the time we get done, it will have passed on over us."

"Or maybe not. We parked at the far end of the lot, if it keeps up and gets worse, we could get soaked. While it's still just spitting down, maybe I should go get our umbrellas. Just in case."

"Don't bother," Eugene said and pointed to a display right outside the café area. "They have umbrellas for sale if it comes to that."

"No need to waste money on new umbrellas when we have perfectly good ones in the car. You go ahead and get in line; I'll run out and grab them."

"No. If you insist on getting the umbrellas, I'll go."

Helen reached up and put a hand against her husband's cheek. Her skin felt like thin parchment, brittle and fragile. "I may not have another chance to walk through a spring rain."

Eugene felt his heart swelling and breaking simultaneously. He leaned forward and kissed his wife. She'd lost so much weight, her clothes hung on her like she was a coatrack instead of an actual person, but she was still beautiful to him. "Hurry back, love."

As he stepped to the rear of the line, he watched his wife walk through the café and the store itself, exiting through the front doors that led onto the parking lot. Only seconds later, the drizzle became a downpour, beating on the pavement outside with a staccato percussion that sounded like an army of galloping horses.

"Christ on a cracker," he mumbled under his breath. "She's going to get drenched."

12:25pm

As Vincent turned the car into the parking lot, the rain really started to come down. So hard that it completely obstructed his view out the windshield. He flipped on the wipers, expecting them to clear the glass—but instead, they had the opposite effect. The water didn't slide off as the blades swiped back and forth; instead it *smeared.* Not like water at all, or even a liquid. More like some viscous jelly coating his windshield with a gloopy membrane.

The world outside the car became nothing more than an indistinct blur, almost as if he were looking at everything through a veil of mucus, but he spotted an empty space and made for it. He stomped on the brakes when a skinny old woman struggling with an umbrella seemed to materialize out of nowhere. She waved and scuttled on.

Vincent pulled into the space, cut the engine, then sat there for a moment, mesmerized by the rain that wasn't exactly rain collecting on the windshield, now running down the glass in slimy globs.

"What the hell is this stuff?" he asked himself. Of course there was no answer forthcoming.

The store was only a few feet away, but he didn't really fancy getting out of the car while a snot-storm raged. He didn't have an umbrella with him, and he didn't want to end up looking like something from one of those *Alien* movies by the time he made it to the store.

He let a few more minutes pass, hoping the rain would let up. When it continued unabated, he considered calling Tony and telling him he couldn't get out of the car. He could just hear Tony's response: "*You're canceling our lunch date because you don't want to get your hair wet?*"

But it wasn't just getting wet; it was getting slimed. Then a wicked little voice in the back of his head asked if he'd be willing to risk it if it was Raul's talented mouth waiting for him.

Maybe he deserved to be covered in slime, his outsides matching his insides.

"Fuck it," he said, reaching into the back to grab the jacket he hadn't taken out of the car since winter. He threw the jacket over his head, popped open the door, and made a mad dash across the parking lot.

12:26pm

Dena and her mother had come straight into the store, but her dad lingered outside to chat with a worker who was fishing a bicycle out of the lake. No doubt some fraternity prank or dare, Dena figured.

It was typical behavior for her dad to strike up a conversation with a complete stranger. Happened everywhere they went, without fail. Walmart, the movies, hotel lobby while on vacation. He never met anyone with whom he couldn't find something to converse about, viewing everyone he encountered as a potential buddy. Dena found it kind of annoying, but also kind of endearing.

As her mother checked out a rack of T-shirts, Dena zeroed in on an adorable crop top that she thought would look so cute on her. Of course, her parents would raise a ruckus about it. They never liked her to show too much skin. Here she was preparing to become a college woman, and they were still treating her as if she were two days out of kindergarten.

Screw it, she thought. It was her money, and she was a young adult, not a child. She was going to get the crop top, to hell with what her parents had to say about it.

Her mother stepped up next to her, and Dena braced herself for a lecture on dressing trashy. But instead, her mother said, “What’s that noise? Is that rain?”

Dena tilted her head to listen and realized she could hear something beating on the roof, had been hearing it for a couple of minutes in fact without it truly registering consciously. She craned her neck, but from this corner of the space she couldn’t see the windows at the front of the store or by the café.

“If it is, Dad is going to be soaking wet.”

And then she saw him, shuffling down the center aisle that led from the entrance back to the registers and customer service window. He moved stiffly, with his arms held away from his body. He was indeed soaked . . . or something. As he got closer and spotted them, turning to head their way, Dena saw that the rain wasn’t so much dripping off him as it was hanging in globs and stringy ropes.

“Jerry, what happened to you?” her mother exclaimed. “Did you fall in the lake or something?”

"No, this is from the rain."

Dena scrunched up her nose. Her dad smelled like rotting fish; no wonder her mother thought he'd fallen in the lake. "That doesn't look like rainwater, Dad."

"It isn't. I don't know what it is. Some kind of gelatinous blobs, that's what's raining down out there."

"That doesn't make any sense," Dena's mother said with a frown.

"Look at me, Penny. The proof is all over me. But if you want more evidence, feel free to go take a look out the door. Only I don't recommend you walk out in it."

Dena started toward the front of the store, but then her dad pointed to her hands and said, "What's that?"

She looked down, only now realizing that she still held the crop top. "Oh, just something I was thinking of buying."

"No!" her parents said in unison.

12:27pm

People were getting out of line to go stare at the rain through the windows. Pamela had to admit, she was a bit intrigued by the unexpected rain herself, considering that she had just been wishing for it shortly before it started. But these people were gawking and murmuring as if they'd never seen precipitation before. A bunch of Chicken Littles, astounded by the falling sky.

She'd seen a handful of people come into the store out of the rain, one little old lady trekking through the café on her way to the bathrooms. That meant more of a mess they'd have to clean up after closing tonight.

She handed a vanilla bean frap to a customer and noticed even more people leaving the line to stare out the window.

"What are they looking at?" Jessica asked.

"I don't know. Hold down the fort for a minute, I'm going to check it out."

Before Jessica could argue about being left to man the café alone, even if for only a moment, Pamela walked out from around the counter. Her foot landed in something slippery and she nearly toppled over, grabbing hold of a display of Cliff bars to keep herself upright. Looking down, expecting to find spilled coffee, instead she saw some kind of thick, clear goo on the floor. It gave off an unpleasant odor. No idea what it was, but disgusted that it was now on her shoe, she continued over to the windows.

"What's so interesting outside?" she asked, but no one had to answer her. This close up, she could see it for herself.

The rain outside, coming down onto the pavement of the courtyard and into the churning waters of the lake, wasn't rain as she'd ever seen it. It seemed too solid—and for a moment, she wondered if it might be hail. Only when it impacted the ground, it sort of exploded, like water balloons. The drops that hit the window streaked down slowly, leaving a slimy residue like slug trails. Lightning flashed in the clouds every few seconds, but there was no accompanying thunder.

"What's happening?" said a woman to Pamela's right.

"Only one way to find out," said a male student who Pamela recognized but couldn't name. He pushed through the door and held his hand out into the rain, letting some of it plop into his palm. He made a face, gagged, then rubbed his hand furiously against his pant leg, allowing the door to swing shut.

"What is it?" Pamela asked.

"Beats me, but whatever it is, it's gross, Like some kind of snot balls or something." He continued to rub his hand against his leg.

An older man who came by the café every day for a banana nut muffin said, "I read that sometimes a plane will accidentally drop the contents of its toilets in mid-flight."

"You mean I just got a handful of airliner shit?" the student said, gagging again.

Multiple people began talking loudly, their voices strident, but Pamela clapped her hands together sharply to get everyone's attention. "Come on, if that was the case then it wouldn't be a continuous rain. It would have simply splashed down on us and been done."

"Then what is it?" Mr. Banana Nut Muffin said, parroting her earlier question.

Pamela stared back out the window but didn't answer. Truth was, she didn't know.

12:28pm

Tony found the maroon-and-white Friedkin beach towels in the back, took one to the customer service window, and handed it to Vincent. His husband used the towel to start wiping the gooey substance off his face and neck.

Yolanda, hovering nearby, said, "I don't think we're supposed to use stock like that."

"I'll pay for it later," Tony said then turned back to Vincent. "And you said that gunk is just falling right out of the sky?"

"Like this is an episode of *You Can't Do That On Television* and I said, 'I don't know'."

"What?" Yolanda said.

Vincent directed a tight smile her way. "Pop culture reference before your time, sweetie."

"What is that stuff?" Tony asked.

"Damned if I know. It's kind of got the slippery consistency of lube."

"Well, somehow I seriously doubt that it's raining lube."

"According to the Weather Girls, it was raining men once, so wouldn't lube be the next logical item to follow?"

A laugh sputtered past Tony's lips. That was one of the things he loved most about Vincent; no matter the situation, he could always make Tony laugh.

Vincent wiped at his clothes with the towel, but the towel itself had become saturated with the gunk, and a sticky, slimy puddle had formed around his feet. "You got another one of these?"

"Yeah, I'll be right back," he said, and then to Yolanda, "I'll pay for both of them."

When he returned with the second towel, he found Vincent staring at his cell phone with a frown.

"Did it get ruined?"

Vincent looked up, and for a fraction of a second Tony thought he detected the guilty look of a child caught jumping on the sofa when he'd been told not to. Then Vincent's expression evened out and Tony figured he'd only startled his husband. "No, I was worried about that, but it seems to be fine."

"Good," Tony said, then spotted a family of three near the front of the store. The father seemed to have gotten slimed as well. Tony began to feel the first tendrils of real unease snaking from his gut up toward his throat, like vines creeping up a trellis. What could this substance raining down over campus be, and was there any possibility it might be toxic? "You didn't get any of that gunk in your mouth, did you?"

Vincent froze as he wiped his pants with the second towel, and Tony could see the same unease suddenly flooding his husband. "No, at least I don't think I did. You don't suppose this stuff . . . ?"

Tony pulled out his own phone. "Maybe we should see if there's anything about this on the news."

12:30pm

Eugene knocked again at the restroom door. "Helen, you sure you're okay?"

"I told you I'd be right out," she called through the door.

While he waited, he glanced back down the short hallway to the crowd gathered at the windows. He'd given up his place in line, but the line itself had disintegrated as everyone became fixated on the strange sludgy rain outside.

When Helen had breezed past him a few minutes ago, saying she wanted to get cleaned up in the restroom, he'd noticed something odd about the rain that covered her but hadn't had the time to really examine it as she disappeared down the little hall. Now that he realized what fell outside was no ordinary rain, he found himself worrying almost as much as when she'd discovered that first lump on her left breast.

The floor leading down the hall to the restroom door was slick with globs of the sludge which had no doubt dripped off Helen as she made her way here. It stank to high heaven, reminding him vaguely of his childhood and the days his mother would leave a big pot of salmon stew simmering on the stove. Eugene found himself stepping around the puddles, not wanting to touch it directly.

When the door opened and Helen stepped out, Eugene moved to hug her . . . then halted. Her thinning white hair was slicked back like some 1930s gangster. Her face shone with a ruddy glow as if she'd just scrubbed it furiously, and her blouse and pants were glistening wet but also stiff, as if some tacky substance were drying on them. Again, he was taken back to childhood and his mother complaining about his 'stiff sheets'. At the thought, he felt his own face grow ruddy with heat.

"I gave myself a birdbath in the sink," Helen said. "Think I got all that stuff off my skin and out of my hair, and I did the best I could to wipe it off my clothes with paper towels. But there was only so much I could do there."

Eugene glanced down at a puddle next to his foot, then back up to his wife. "Any idea what this sludge is?"

"Not a clue. I tried to shield myself as much as possible with one of the umbrellas, but the stuff kept blowing up underneath it. By the time I made it back to the store, I was pretty much covered head to toe in it and I had to ditch both umbrellas in the trash. Seems

I left a trail like Hansel and Gretel if they had slime balls instead of breadcrumbs."

"Don't worry, they'll clean that up," Eugene said, reaching out and taking his wife's hand. He did so tentatively, almost hesitantly. He found the substance so revolting that he didn't want to touch even a hem of Helen's clothing, where the residue remained. "Come on, let's go grab that sandwich."

Helen shook her head. "Maybe I'll take a hot tea, but I'm not really hungry anymore. In fact, I'm feeling a little queasy all of a sudden."

12:32pm

As Lisa Kline neared the bookstore, she decided that would be her destination instead of the dining hall. She'd noticed the clouds as she left the Conference Center near the gymnasium, where she'd be helping with the final edits of the TEDx Talks Friedkin had hosted this past February, but hadn't worried about any impending precipitation. She didn't mind a sprint in the rain, and her grumbling stomach told her she didn't have time to swing by the dorm to pick up her umbrella.

The rain had started falling only minutes after she started out, and she could tell instantly that something wasn't right with the big flat drops that plopped onto her head. She reached up and felt something slimy in her hair. For a moment she thought maybe a bird had relieved itself on her head, but then she noticed the drops falling around her weren't regular rain—but globules of some kind. She picked up speed, her trot turning to a jog turning to an actual run. She ducked her head down, but that didn't prevent her from becoming thoroughly coated in the globs in a matter of seconds.

She briefly considered changing course and heading for her room in Tremblay Hall instead. No food there, other than some chips and candy bars in the snack machine, but it did have a shower and a change of clothes. By that point, she was closer to the lake than the dorms though and decided to just keep going to the dining hall. However, the bookstore rose up like a refuge. She could take shelter from this strange storm, and there would be food in the café.

She came to a stop under the overhang just outside the main entrance, panting and wrinkling her nose at the fishy smell of the globs that now clung to her like a new layer of skin. Closing her eyes, she shook her head like a dog and then waved her hands back and forth to get as much of the crap off as she could. Then she clawed at her face to clean it.

In the end, she felt like she'd done little more than smear the crap around. Opening the door, she stepped inside to find the store fairly packed, with people having clumped together in three main groups. One right in front of her on the other side of the fireplace; one in the café near the counter; one at the back of the store by the registers.

She saw what drew them all like moths to a candle. The television monitors. The one nearest her was showing some asinine talk show with the volume turned down, but even as she watched, the channel switched to CNN and the volume came up, the news blasting out.

Excerpt from *The Day the Rains Came: An Annotated Timeline of the Deluge*

FOR THE SAKE of this timeline, I will give all times in Eastern Standard Time (with the local time of each site in parenthesis after) since the first rain started on the east coast of the United States.

The second rain started at 12:24:02pm (6:24:02pm) in Gubbio, Italy. The next at 12:25:14pm (6:25:14pm) in Reine, Norway. The next at 12:26:28pm (8:26:28pm) in Bryansk, Russia.

Initially, the rain would begin to fall in a new location approximately every minute, though not exact. The first four locations were all small towns that the average person would never have heard of. Why that should be, and what significance that might have, remain another of the Deluge's many mysteries.

Then at 12:27:52pm (1:27:52pm), it began to rain in Buenos Aires, Argentina. At 12:28:14pm (12:28:14am) in Beijing, China. At 12:29:03pm (3:29:03am) in Sydney, Australia. At 12:29:50pm (8:29:50am) in Anchorage, United States.

Here we will pause to point out the significance of the rainfall in the Alaskan city of Anchorage. What this showed was that even in climes where the frigid temperatures should have crystalized the rain into ice or snow, the substance remained the same gelatinous consistency as in warmer regions. It also marked the fact that the phenomenon was speeding up.

12:35pm

AFTER CHANGING THE channels on the television monitors, and turning up the volume to broadcast through the intercom system that typically played easy listening, Pamela left the cash room in the back where the controls for all the electronic equipment were housed and returned to the store.

Behind the registers, Tony and Yolanda stood gazing at the monitor. Across the counter were a group of half a dozen customers, including Tony's husband. Tony had briefly introduced them after he'd called Pamela over and told her about what he'd read on his phone. She had decided it would be best to get the news up for everyone to see.

As she took her place behind her two employees, a news anchor with architecturally-coifed hair and a neutral expression appeared on screen and began laying it out for everyone.

"For those just joining us, we continue to monitor the unprecedented meteorological event which seems to be happening throughout the world. At present, we have confirmed that in eighteen different cities in fifteen different countries, a so-far unidentified substance is raining down. The substance is thick and gummy. We are not even sure at this early stage if the substance is water-based." Here the anchor paused, putting a hand up to her ear, obviously listening to

someone speaking to her through an earpiece. "*I'm being told that we have confirmed six new cities reporting the rain, with more possible but not yet confirmed. You'll see the names of the confirmed cities on the scroll at the bottom of your screen. Folks, you'll have to bear with us. This is all unfolding in real-time, and we are doing our best to provide you with developments as they occur. Apparently in Washington D.C., where it started to rain just a moment ago, members of the Agricultural Department have mobilized to collect samples of the material and examine it. This is also happening in Atlanta, headquarters of the Centers for Disease Control and Prevention. In fact, I think we have someone from the CDC on the line to tell us what steps they are taking . . .*"

"The CDC," Yolanda said, turning to Pamela. "Why would they be getting involved?"

Pamela didn't answer immediately. Partly because she didn't know for sure, but also because the guesses she could make had implications she didn't really want to consider.

Dr. Argentine, an English Lit professor for the university, used her hesitation to further his own opinion. "Perhaps they suspect the substance may contain some kind of bacterial contagion."

This led to some gasps and panicked chatter among the customers, but Pamela raised her voice and said, "That is speculation, and I suggest we don't get worked up about this until we know more."

"Could be biological warfare," said a middle-aged customer with a balding head and an expanding gut. "I always knew it was only a matter of time before somebody tried to wipe us out with some kind of manmade virus. The Chinese tried a few years ago with that Corona thing but failed, so maybe they're trying again."

Great, Pamela thought. *A conspiracy nut. Just what we need.*

A male student wearing a maroon tee with the school's knight mascot on the front, laughed. "It's happening all over the world, on every single continent."

"Could be it got loose like in that Stephen King book," the balding customer said.

"But how could they make it rain everywhere?" asked an older woman. "I mean, terrorists can't control the weather, can they? Although I do remember one time on *General Hospital*—"

"Everyone calm down," Tony said in a voice that was firm but reassuring, and Pamela could have kissed him in that moment. "We'll just leave the news on. No reason to start spinning crazy theories when they'll let us know any important information."

Baldy, as Pamela started to think of him, grumbled under his breath, something about "fake news" and "should be watching FOX News", but he didn't share this with the group at large.

Tony's husband, Vincent she thought his name was, held out his arms, two slimed towels in each hand. "Biological warfare or not," he said, "I can't stay in these clothes."

"Is it okay if he picks out an outfit and changes in the bathroom?" Tony asked Pamela. "I'll pay for that and the towels."

Pamela smiled at Vincent. "Certainly. We don't

have much to offer in terms of couture, but we have an endless supply of hoodies and sweatpants."

"Any port in a storm," Vincent said, returning her smile before heading out further into the store.

Yolanda, wringing her hands so hard Pamela feared the young woman might tie her fingers in knots, said, "I'm off at two, but I don't know that I should go out in that stuff."

Pamela put her hands on the girl's shoulders. "Relax. Like Tony said, let's just watch the news, see what they have to say."

The radio, still in Tony's hand, squawked with static, then Jessica's voice called, "Pamela?"

Pamela glanced toward the café and saw that people had started to reform the line. Perhaps it said something about the human spirit that even in the face of circumstances that could not be explained and could potentially be dangerous, people still needed their fancy coffee drinks and baked goods.

Of course, Pamela thought as she headed toward the café, she wasn't sure if what that said about the human spirit was positive or negative.

12:37pm

Thomas Argentine stuck near the registers, waiting for Tony to get done with a conversation with the cashier. Just as the young man turned to head into the back, Thomas stepped forward and said, "Crazy stuff, huh?"

"Something right out of *The X-Files*, Dr., um, Dr . . . "

"Argentine. We've spoken a few times."

"Yes, I know. I'm just terrible with names, don't take it personally."

"No problem, and you can feel free to call me Thomas."

"I will. I'm—"

"Tony," Thomas said. "I remember."

Tony nodded then glanced around. Silently, Thomas cursed his own awkwardness. Not really having anything else to say but not wanting the conversation to end so soon, he said, "I like your shirt."

Tony looked down at what he was wearing. A simple light blue button-up. Nice enough, but Thomas had to admit there was nothing all that special or noteworthy about it. Thomas also had to admit that not only was he bad at this, he was ridiculously obvious.

"Well," Tony said after another moment of uncomfortable silence, "I should get back to work."

"I'll stay out here and man the television. I'll let you know if they report anything important."

"Thanks. I've never heard of anything like this happening before."

"Actually—"

"So, do I look like the world's biggest dork or what?"

Thomas glanced over to see Tony's sleazy husband walking up, wearing a gray hoodie with 'FU' across the front and matching sweatpants with 'FRIEDKIN' written down the side.

Tony gazed at his husband with a smile. "I'd say you look like a man with an overabundance of school spirit for a school you didn't even go to."

"There are a few others who got slimed that I think

are going to be doing the same thing, so one silver lining to this shit is that you'll sell some clothes you might not have otherwise."

"My husband, always with the glass-is-half-full outlook."

The two shared a laugh, and Thomas wanted to vomit. Instead, he forced a laugh of his own.

"Oh, Vincent," Tony said, seeming to remember that the professor was there, "meet Dr. Argentine—um, Thomas."

Vincent glanced Thomas's way and gave a dismissive nod before turning his attention back to Tony. "So you still want to grab something to eat? I'm certainly not going anywhere until this rain stops."

"Sure. Go get in line, I'll clock out for lunch and meet you over at the café."

Vincent started toward the café, and Tony into the back, neither of them acknowledging Thomas or saying so much as 'See you later'.

Feeling hollow inside, the way he used to feel way back in high school when he had to sit alone at a table during lunch, Thomas wandered back up to the front of the store and took a chair by the fireplace. He saw a family of three in the Nike section, obviously looking for something for the father, who was coated in the slimy gunk.

Over at the café, Pamela manned the counter while Jessica, who handled textbooks, mopped up some more of the gunk from the floor.

Thomas knew his focus should be on this bizarre weather phenomenon, but instead his mind fixed resolutely on Tony. The man was adorable and seemed so sweet and gentle. After their first conversation the day Tony had started at the store, brief as it was, Thomas had done a little social media stalking. Turned out he and Tony shared the love of a lot of the same books, and movies, and TV shows. A crush began to form. A doomed crush on a married man, but one can't control their feelings. And then today Thomas had gotten a glimpse of Tony's husband, Vincent, and had instantly recognized him. The two had never met in person, and before today Thomas had only known him by the name 'BigDickDriver'.

Thomas considered himself a romantic, and since his partner Earl had passed away eight years ago, he had hoped to find someone new to love, to share a life with . . . and yet he still had needs and desires. Which led him to visit internet hookup sites from time to time.

It was on one of these sites that Thomas had begun exchanging messages with BigDickDriver. The talk had been hot and steamy and progressed far enough for them to exchange pictures. Thomas had found BDD incredibly sexy, but apparently BDD hadn't liked what he saw, because he stopped responding to messages and ended up blocking Thomas.

And he had no doubt that Vincent was BigDickDriver. He didn't seem to recognize Thomas at all, which suggested he was on the site so often and saw so many pictures that they all blurred together. So now Thomas was left with a dilemma. The man he had a crush on was married to a cheater. Should he tell what he knew? Then again, what did he really know? He hadn't saved the picture so he didn't have proof, and who was to say that Vincent had ever actually hooked up with anyone from the site? He could be one of those types that got off on talking dirty online and 'collecting photos' but never actually going through and meeting anyone in person. Of course, that still made him a creep—but it didn't make him a cheat.

Unable to determine the best thing to do, Thomas did nothing but sit in the chair, the hollowness inside becoming an ache as he wished that Earl were still here.

12:52pm

Lisa rummaged through the clearance racks, trying to find something she could afford to change into. She was a college student on a tight budget, and her bank account was a bit anorexic until the beginning of next month when her father would deposit an allowance he could ill afford himself.

She still couldn't believe she was here, at such an expensive university. But, being salutatorian of her high school class, plus the low income her father made at the hardware store, had actually helped them weave together a flimsy quilt of scholarships and need-based grants so that she had just enough to make this a possibility for her.

"Damn," she muttered once she'd gone through both racks and found no sweatpants. There were a few pairs of Under Armor running shorts. Though even the discounted price was over thirty bucks, they would have to do. Coupled with the ten-dollar tee she'd found, it would damn near break her—but she had to get out of these fouled clothes. She'd cleaned herself off in the bathroom as well as she could, but a new outfit was a necessity.

As she pulled a pair of shorts off the rack, she glanced back toward the windows. The rain fell unabated, showing no signs of stopping or even slackening. According to the TV around the corner, three-fourths of the world was experiencing the rain now. Made no sense; even scientists were baffled. The President of the United States kept saying not to worry, his administration had the situation under control, but he said that about everything, even things that clearly were out of control and should inspire worry. She was not reassured.

She pulled out her phone and tried calling her father again. For the third time, his answering machine picked up. She still couldn't believe he didn't have a cellphone in this day and age, though she suspected the fact that he paid for hers and gave her a monthly allowance had more to do with that than an old-fogey distrust of modern technology.

She walked to the back of the store and paid for her items, doing some mental calculations and figuring out that this left her with only seventeen dollars. Luckily it was nearly the end of the month and her bank account would get a little extra padding from her father soon.

Back in the bathroom, she stripped out of her clothes, and after a brief consideration just stuffed them in the wastebasket. She suspected no amount of washing would ever get that stink out. She slipped on the tee and squeezed into shorts, which were much tighter and shorter than anything she normally would wear. When her phone rang, trilling a Taylor Swift tune, she let out a startled squeak then laughed at her own jumpiness.

Seeing the caller ID, she snatched the phone from the sink where she'd left it. "Daddy?"

"Hey baby, how you holding up?"

"Worried sick about you, that's how I'm holding up. I called you three times. I know you aren't working today, so where have you been?"

"You know I'm not a shut-in or a recluse, right? Even when I'm not working, I occasionally have to leave the house. Just got back from making a grocery run."

"Do you know what's going on?" Lisa asked, lowering the lid of the toilet and taking a seat.

"Yes, it's all over the radio. I saw you called when I got home, but I was going to be calling you first thing anyway. Didn't even take the time to bring in the groceries yet. Are you okay? Are you safe?"

"Um . . . yeah."

"What's wrong? You know I can always tell by your voice when something's wrong."

Lisa hesitated, took a deep breath, then said, "I got caught out in it. I got to the bookstore and I'm all cleaned up now and I changed clothes, but I did get pretty drenched."

Now it was her father's turn to hesitate. "Well, so far they haven't found anything *wrong* with the rain other than it being a weird consistency. I'm sure there's nothing to worry about."

"So the President keeps telling us."

"What?"

"Nothing," Lisa said with a soft laugh. Just hearing her father's voice made her feel better, less anxious. She wished if this had to have happened, it could have waited until summer when they would be together.

Since her mother died when she was ten, it had been just her and her father, the Dynamic Duo as he sometimes called them. He was her hero and her rock.

"It's not raining here yet," her father said. "Guess this little Podunk town in Virginia is too out of the way even for a mystery rain."

"Daddy, promise me you won't go back out. It didn't seem like it was going to rain here until the minute before it started. Maybe there isn't anything harmful about this, but I'll feel a lot better knowing that you're not out in it."

"I promise. As soon as I get the groceries out of the car, I'll—"

"Daddy?" Lisa called when he didn't say anything more for several seconds. She checked the screen of her phone to make sure the call hadn't dropped. His words had cut off so abruptly. "Daddy, are you there?"

"Sorry, yes baby, I'm here. I glanced out the front door and . . . well, it just started to rain here."

1:15pm

Dena's dad looked ridiculous in the baggy sweatpants and the 'FU Dad' t-shirt, and under normal circumstances she would be mercilessly teasing him about his appearance.

But these weren't normal circumstances.

Her dad had bought them some food from the café, and they sat at a round table in the far corner of the area, just past the convenience items, as far from the windows as they could get. In fact, Dena sat with her back to the windows so she didn't have to see the rain.

Instead, she kept throwing anxious glances at her dad.

He caught her staring again, swallowed a bite of muffin, and said, "For the hundredth time, I'm fine."

"But it was all over you," Dena said.

"You heard what they said on the news," her mother chimed in, though her expression and tone evinced more worry than her words. "They've found nothing toxic in the samples they've studied so far."

Yes, Dena had heard that, but she also knew that it was early in the process and they were still doing tests. And while they hadn't found anything toxic, what they had found only made the rain more mystifying. For instance, the main component that seemed to make up the substance raining down outside was human lymphocytes. It made no sense, and despite a lot of talking heads putting forth various theories, no one seemed to know much that was definite. All they knew for sure was that it was now raining everywhere in the world.

"The government is urging people to stay indoors and not go out in it," Dena said, unable to let go of this. "Why would they do that if they weren't afraid this could be dangerous?"

Her dad reached across to take her hand, but stopped at the last minute and returned his hand to his lap. "They're just being cautious."

Dena nodded and looked down at the uneaten muffin on the plate before her. She didn't have much of an appetite at the moment. She was worried about her dad, yes, but she also felt like a shitty jerk for being angry that this situation had marred her visit to the campus.

She'd experienced a similar dichotomy of emotion after her dad's heart attack. Of course she'd been terribly worried for his wellbeing, but she also had to admit that a petty part of her had been annoyed by the inconvenience the timing had brought to her own life. She supposed such a thing was only natural, but she still felt like a bad person.

"So, do you still want that crop top?" Dena's mother asked.

Dena looked up. "Okay, now I know things are dire if you're willing to let me get that shirt."

"I didn't say I liked it or approved. But you're right, you're a young woman now and you earned that money babysitting. Have to let you start making your own decisions sometimes."

"Even when they are the wrong decisions," her dad added.

Dena tried on a smile but it wilted quickly.

Her dad suddenly sneezed three times in rapid succession—the powerful kind that seemed almost like explosions.

"Jeez," he said, "I hope I'm not catching a cold."

Her mother placed a palm again his forehead. "You might be a little warm, hard to tell. Want me to go buy you one of the jackets?"

"At these prices, no thanks," her dad said with a laugh. "We spent enough on this utterly absurd ensemble."

This time, Dena's smile caught and she even let loose with a small laugh herself.

From somewhere behind her, Dena heard someone gasp and a chair scrape against the floor. She looked over her shoulder to see an athletic young man standing, gaping down at his phone. “Holy shit!” he exclaimed. “Guys, I just saw on Facebook that someone caught out in the rain in Arizona has died.”

Dena immediately spun back around in her seat to look at her dad.

“I was afraid of this,” said an older man in tan slacks and a paisley polo, walking into the café from the bookstore area. “I remember reading that a comparable phenomenon happened around about twenty-five years ago, a similar type of rain although it only affected this one town in Washington State. From what I recall, it made all the townspeople sick.”

A silence of about ten to fifteen seconds followed this announcement, and then Dena’s dad sneezed again.

Excerpt from *The Day the Rains Came: An Annotated Timeline of the Deluge*

REFERENCES TO THE similar rain that fell on Oakville, Washington, on August 7th of 1994 began to pop up on various social media sites and blogs within the first forty-five minutes of the Deluge. However, this was not reported on any mainstream media sites or networks until nearly an hour after the first reporting of the phenomenon in Greenville, South Carolina. Several journalists and meteorologists interviewed for this book reported a similar motivation for not mentioning this sooner: there was no proven connection between the two incidents, and the media did not want to incite a panic.

The biggest similarity between the two incidents was the consistency of the rain itself, the almost mucus-like quality, and the fact that no one could figure out exactly what caused it.

However, the dissimilarities are greater. The rain in Oakville lasted for only a few hours and was confined to one general location. Conspiracy theorists who believe the rain was a governmental bioweapon (though which government varies depending on the theorist), or even a product of an alien civilization, have conjectured that Oakville was a trial run, a testing ground for the Deluge. There is, of course, no evidence of this.

Another feature of the rain that fell over the Washington town in 1994 is that it contained some form of bacteria that made the townspeople who came into contact with it sick with flu-like symptoms, a sickness that lasted three to six weeks. There were no reported deaths from this.

When Orlando Granger, aged forty-nine, passed away in his home in Phoenix, Arizona, less than half an hour after making contact with the rain on April 24, 20—, the caution and restraint of the media was not enough to prevent the panic that began to sweep the globe.

1:30pm

PAMELA RUBBED AT her temples, the mingling of a dozen or more raised voices causing a pounding like a snare drum in her head. She knew they were all looking to her as some sort of *de facto* leader because she was the store manager, but she hadn't signed on for this. The hardest decisions she usually had to make were whether or not to accept back a textbook rental with slight water damage, and what to do with all the Saint Patrick's Day shirts that didn't sell.

"Everyone, pause!" she shouted, her voice strident and only causing her headache to worsen.

Almost everyone in the store, probably close to thirty people, had congregated near the customer service window, most of them angry. She found herself flashing on the scene at the end of the old Elizabeth Taylor movie *Suddenly Last Summer*, where a mob literally tears a guy limb from limb.

Her high-pitched shout did cut through the din, and the crowd quieted, at least momentarily. Now they were all looking at her as if she had some kind of answers, but all she had was a budding migraine.

"I know everyone is scared," she said, trying to imagine this was a movie and there was inspirational music swelling in the background as she gave words of comfort and assurance. "But let's not go crazy, okay? There is sketchy news about the guy in Phoenix, nothing definite from any of the major networks. We don't even know if the rain had anything to do with his death."

Voices began to rise again, her speech failing to inspire. If this was a movie, apparently it was some cheap Lifetime original with Candace Cameron Bure playing her.

Baldy, not surprisingly, outshouted everyone else. "So you think it's mere coincidence that a man died right after coming into contact with that slimy stuff?"

"It could very well be a coincidence," Tony spoke up, stepping up next to her. "One case isn't enough to draw any conclusions. As Pamela said, we don't have any definitive information yet."

"What about what Dr. Argentine told us?" Yolanda said. "This has happened before."

All eyes turned to the professor, and Pamela found herself wishing the man had kept his big mouth shut. Her contact with him suggested he always needed to feel like the smartest man in the room and was therefore always in lecture mode, even on subjects of which he knew little.

In his defense, Dr. Argentine's expression at the sudden scrutiny suggested he also wished he'd kept his big mouth shut.

"I didn't mean to suggest the two events are

identical," he stammered. "I mean, superficially there are similarities, but that's not enough to make any concrete determinations."

"That guy sneezed," Baldy said, pointing at an older man with his family.

"It's allergy season," Pamela said, concerned with the group of five that gathered loosely around Baldy and seemed to be nodding at everything he said. "People sneeze, that doesn't mean anything."

Tony tried again to add his voice of reason. "Look, even if this is something similar to what happened in 1994, no one died from that."

"Yeah, but someone already died from *this*," said a young lady who Pamela thought worked in the campus post office located in the Malerman Center next door. She was one of the ones gathered around Baldy.

"Again, we don't know why that man died," Pamela said. "The people here were exposed to the rain before it even started raining in Phoenix, and sneezing aside, everyone seems to be fine."

Baldy laughed, the sound low and nasty. "*Seems to be* being the operative phrase. This is an unknown contagion; it could have different incubation periods for different hosts. And I don't want this guy anywhere near me."

"Stop talking about my dad like he's got the plague!" shouted the teenaged girl with the man Baldy kept pointing to. "There's nothing wrong with him."

"Maybe not," Baldy said, lowering his voice to make himself sound reasonable, which was more dangerous in Pamela's estimation than his raving. "But as we keep being told, we don't know anything definite. Maybe the people who've been exposed are fine . . . but maybe they're not. Do we really want to risk it?"

"What do you suggest?" Yolanda asked, and Pamela wanted to fire her on the spot for humoring this fear-monger.

Baldy scratched his chin as if giving the question deep thought. "Remember the Corona thing? How did we get through it? Self-isolation. Quarantine. We just need to prevent further exposure for the rest of us."

"You're not proposing we send them outside, are you?" Dr. Argentine asked, seemingly horrified by the prospect. But all Pamela could think was, *You helped start this, intentionally or not, you asshole.*

Baldy shook his head. "Probably won't come to that. There's a little area around the corner by the school supplies that I think would do. Just put them over there, at least until we know more."

"That sounds reasonable," the post office worker said.

And, Pamela thought, that was how all great evil spread . . . by sounding reasonable. Still, this wasn't Nazi Germany, and no one was being thrown into gas chambers.

Addressing the crowd as a whole, but specifically those who had come into contact with the rain, she said, "Okay guys, would those who were caught out in the rain be willing to *voluntarily* self-isolate for now?"

The man who had been the focus of Baldy's attention, the conspicuous sneezer, said, "Sure, I will."

His daughter began to cry. "Dad, no."

"It's fine, honey. I'll be right over there, no big deal."

"We should make the families go with them," Baldy said loudly. "They may have gotten some of the stuff on them."

"No," Pamela said, impressed by how firm and authoritative the word came out. "We're not *making* anyone do anything. If they want to self-isolate, that's fine, but we're not forcing them to go. And if families want to go with them, that's fine too, but it's all voluntary."

"I'll go," said a girl Pamela recognized as a student. "You know, to be on the safe side."

Tony's husband also nodded. "Me too."

"I'll come with you," Tony said.

"You don't have to. Keep working, it's no big deal."

"I'm going with you, dad," the sneezer's daughter said.

"I think you should keep browsing the store," the man said, his voice trying for a breezy calm, but Pamela could see the worry in his face.

He's afraid Baldy might be right.

"I *am* going with you," an older man said to his wife, who had also gotten caught in the rain. Unlike the others, she hadn't bought a new outfit, had instead tried to clean her clothes in the restroom. "And no arguments."

His wife didn't seem like she had any arguments, merely smiled gratefully.

"What about you?" Baldy said, turning to the male student who had stuck his hand out into the rain earlier.

"Hey man, I didn't get drenched or anything. I just got a little bit on my hand and wiped it right off."

"Yeah, and it's still on your pants."

Pamela looked at the boy's leg and saw that Baldy was right. A flaky residue was drying on his jeans.

"Come on, we'll go together," said a young girl in a

ponytail, taking the student's hand. Probably his girlfriend.

Feeling anxious, like this was the start of something that could snowball out of control, Pamela watched as the seven began to make their way over to the school supplies. Halfway there, the sneezer sneezed again. Pamela's headache throbbed.

1:35pm

Vincent paced around for a few minutes, avoiding the other exiles as much as possible, then pulled out his phone and powered it on. He'd had to turn it off earlier because Raul wouldn't stop texting, breaking a cardinal rule of their relationship. Raul was never supposed to initiate texts or calls, ensuring that they only communicated when Vincent knew the coast was clear.

He had over twenty missed texts from Raul. A ridiculous breach of the keeping-it-on-the-down-low parameters they had set to ensure Vincent didn't get caught. He realized these were unusual circumstances, but Raul had known Vincent was on his way to have lunch with Tony, so it still seemed a pretty unforgivable lapse in judgment and sidepiece etiquette.

But he has become more than a mere sidepiece, and you both know it.

Vincent quickly skimmed the texts, all variations on the same theme. *Are you okay? Call me. I'm scared. Are you okay? Call me.*

Vincent shot off a quick text: *What's wrong with you? Trying to get my ass in a sling or what?*

Raul's reply came within a minute: *I'm sorry, I know, but I'm all alone here and the news is freaking me out.*

Vincent felt himself softening, imagining Raul all by himself with no one to talk to. He was a naturally anxious man, easily overwhelmed and much in need of a calming presence. Vincent sometimes mused that this was what had attracted the two of them. Raul needed a strong man to ground him, and Vincent had to admit he had a thing for the wounded in need of a savior.

Vincent peeked around the corner, making sure Tony was nowhere in sight, then took a chance and dialed Raul.

"Vince, baby," Raul said, picking up almost instantaneously. *"Please tell me you're okay."*

"I'm fine, but it sounds like maybe you're not."

"What's going on? I watch all the different news channels, and they all say different things, but no one really seems to know anything. FOX News says that it's all being blown out of proportion."

"Please stop watching FOX News," Vincent said with a chuckle. "I told you, there is no actual news to be found there."

"There's no actual news to be found anywhere, that's what scares me. I read online someone died because of this."

"We only know that someone who was caught in the rain died. We don't know that it was a cause and effect thing."

"But you're okay? Where are you now?"

"Still at the bookstore."

"Good," Raul said, the relief evident in his voice.

"As much as I want you here with me right now, I don't want you to take the chance of going back out in it."

Vincent considered telling Raul that he had been caught in the rain on his way inside, but quickly dismissed the notion. It would only send Raul into a panic.

"Look, I can't talk long. I don't know when Tony might come out from the back again. I'm okay, and I love you."

"I love you too, baby," Raul said.

"Don't message me anymore until I message you, promise?"

"I promise. Just hearing your voice has me feeling better. I might smoke a joint and take a long bath."

"That'll be good for you. I'll talk to you soon."

After they hung up, Vincent immediately deleted the call from the phone's call log, then set about deleting all the texts. He had become quite good in recent months at covering his tracks—a skill he wasn't particularly proud of.

"Excuse me, can I have a moment of your time?"

The voice startled Vincent and he nearly dropped the phone. He turned to find the professor Tony had introduced him to earlier standing a few feet away.

"What is it?" Vincent said, a little more gruffly than he'd intended.

"Do you remember me?" the man asked.

"Yeah, Dr. Arrington, wasn't it?"

"Argentine, actually, but you might know me by a different sobriquet. Does 'LonelyProf' ring a bell?"

Vincent frowned. "What the hell are you babbling about?"

"We chatted before on m4mliaisons-dot-com. Remember?"

A chill quickly spread throughout Vincent's body, freezing him from the inside out. He couldn't say he specifically remembered this guy, certainly not as anyone he'd met in person, but he'd exchanged photos with a lot of men on that website. In fact, it was the one where he'd met Raul.

"I think you have me mistaken for someone else," he finally said. "I've never even heard of that website."

The professor tilted his head, thin lips spreading in a knowing smile. "That so? Who were you talking to on the phone as I was walking over?"

"None of your damn business. I don't know what your trip is, but I'm not whoever you think I am."

"Hmm, my mistake then," Dr. Argentine said, though his expression suggested he didn't think he was mistaken at all.

Vincent didn't say anything more, and the two engaged in a bit of a staring match for another moment before the professor finally turned and walked away. As Vincent watched him go, he had only one thought: *Well, shit. As if things weren't bad enough.*

1:50pm

Charlie Williams woke up disoriented. He rubbed at his eyes and yawned as he tried to push through the sleep-fog that enshrouded his brain. His stomach grumbled, and he thought he should get up and go get breakfast.

Breakfast? Wait, I already had breakfast.

The fog began to dissipate, and Charlie realized he wasn't just waking up from a good night's sleep. In fact, he hadn't slept much at all last night, cramming for the Physics test he had day after tomorrow. He was close to flunking the course, so he had to make at least a B on this upcoming test and the final to even squeak by.

After next-to-no rest, he'd gone to his two morning classes then skipped lunch to come back to his dorm for more studying. He had no afternoon classes, and didn't have to be at work until two. He'd stretched out on his bed with the book on his lap, and his exhaustion had apparently gotten the better of him.

He pushed up onto his elbows, finding that his textbook had fallen onto the floor and his glasses had slipped off onto the pillow. He considered himself lucky he hadn't rolled over and crushed them. Placing the glasses back on his face, he glanced over at the clock on his bedside table, squinting when he didn't at first believe what his eyes told him.

"Holy fuck-balls!" he shouted, jumping up off the bed. If he didn't get his ass in gear right away, he was going to be late for work. Luckily, he was still fully dressed and the café was only a five-minute jog from his dorm. If he hustled, he could make it just in time to avoid being late.

As he slipped on his shoes, he spared a quick glance at Jeffrey's side of the room. Empty, bed undisturbed, as usual. Last month Charlie's roommate had started dating a local girl with her own apartment near downtown, and he'd spent very little time at the dorm since then. Charlie also suspected Jeffrey was spending very little time in class, but that wasn't his business. He wasn't Jeffrey's mother, only his roommate, and barely that these days.

Charlie didn't have time to brush his teeth so he popped in several pieces of gum. As he started for the door, he paused, realizing that he could hear it raining outside. Surprising, since this morning it had been a beautiful sunny day, but he didn't spare much thought on the matter. He grabbed his rain jacket and threw it on, pulling the hood up over his head, then left the room.

On his way to the exit, he passed a few people huddled outside the snack machines. They seemed upset about something, but Charlie didn't have time for collegiate drama. He rushed past them. He realized halfway down the hall that in his hurry he had left his phone back in the room, but he didn't want to waste time going back for it.

He pushed through the door and started running down the paved footpath. He had gotten almost a yard from the dorm before he realized there was something quite peculiar about the rain. It struck his rain slicker with force as if it had some real weight to it, and when drops hit his glasses, they seemed to clump and congeal on the lenses, obscuring his view.

He kept on, his innate distaste for tardiness driving him forward. He prided himself on being reliable and dependable, traits people his age didn't always value, but then Charlie had never been like people his age. It wasn't that he didn't like to have fun, but he also understood his main priority here at Friedkin was to work hard and get that diploma. It probably came from being the first person in his family to get the chance to attend college. He felt he was representing generations of Williamses, and didn't want to let them down. That was the main reason he felt so distraught about doing so poorly in Physics.

All this continued running through Charlie's mind as he approached the bookstore from the back side. He splashed through a puddle that seemed to cling to his shoes as if he were running through oatmeal instead of water.

He typically entered the store from the side entrance which led directly into the café, but today he wanted to get inside as soon as possible. He picked up speed as he neared the main entrance, everything looking distorted through his occluded glasses. A few feet from the door, his left foot slid on something slick that coated the pavement and he pitched forward. Gravity took over after that, and he held his hands out in front of him to break his fall.

He landed in another puddle, his hands and knees sinking into a slimy substance that splashed up into his face as he choked back the gum.

1:57pm

Thomas happened to be standing near the front entrance, staring out the glass of the door, when he saw the figure running toward the bookstore. At first he thought his eyes must be playing tricks on him. The rain had been falling long enough that no one could possibly still be out in it from when it first started, so why would anyone have willingly gone outside during the downpour?

As the figure got closer, he thought he recognized

the baby-faced student that often worked the café. Surely his work ethic wasn't so strong that he would risk his health in order to avoid missing a day of work.

Thomas took an involuntary step toward the door when he saw the young man stumble and fall forward into a puddle. Thomas reached for the door handle then stopped himself. He couldn't go out there. The young man was already covered in the gunk; he would get up and get inside soon enough.

Yet he didn't get up. He remained on his hands and knees, and his body began quaking. The young man seemed in some sort of obvious distress. Thomas couldn't simply stand here and watch without trying to help. Reminding himself that there was an overhang immediately outside this entrance, he grabbed the handle and pulled open the door.

Behind him, he heard someone shout: "What are you doing? Are you crazy?"

Ignoring this, he stepped out, keeping under the overhang, and yelled, "Young man, you need to get inside right away."

The student didn't answer, but he did push up so that he was upright on his knees, clutching at his throat. His body shook as if he were coughing, but Thomas didn't hear any sound.

Choking! The young man is choking!

After that thought, Thomas stopped thinking and began merely reacting. With no consideration of the potential risk and no concern for his own wellbeing, Thomas rushed out into the rain. Instinct took over, and he hurried to the young man, going around to crouch behind him. Thomas wrapped his arms around the student's abdomen. Balling his hands into fists just below the young man's breastbone, Thomas began to press in and up, his First Aid training kicking in as he performed the Heimlich for the first time in his life.

After four of five firm thrusts, a wad of something spat out of the young man's mouth and shot onto the pavement like a projectile. The student whooped air into his lungs and began coughing. He started to sink back onto all fours, but Thomas gripped his arm and yanked him up.

"We can't stay out here," Thomas said directly into the young man's ear and began leading him to the store.

Thomas pulled open the door and practically shoved the young man inside, coming in behind him, for the first time truly becoming aware of the layer of gunk that covered him, running into his eyes and his mouth. He gagged and spat, wiping at his face, then looked up to find everyone in the store had gathered near the entrance. They kept their distance from Thomas and the student, who had gone to his knees and continued coughing—but at least he was breathing.

"Are you suicidal or what?" shouted the bald man who had been raising such a stink since the rain started.

Thomas spit more of the foul-tasting gunk out of his mouth before answering. "This boy was choking out there. I couldn't leave him. That would be inhumane."

"Hey, you signed your own death certificate," the bald man said. "You two gotta go over in the corner with the other ones who've been infected."

"For the last time, we don't know that anyone is

infected with anything," Pamela said, but Thomas couldn't help but note that she didn't suggest that Thomas and the student not go into quarantine, such as it was.

Thomas looked around the crowd, trying to make eye contact with someone who would see reason, but everyone seemed to avoid his gaze, and they continued to back away.

"Fine, whatever," Thomas growled then glanced over at the student. The young man had seemed to recover from his bout of coughing, but the confusion in his eyes was heartbreaking. He clearly didn't know what was going on.

That was why he was out in the rain. He didn't know.

"What's your name, young man?" Thomas asked, popping a squat next to him.

"Ch-charlie. What's going on?"

Thomas held out a hand. "Come with me. I'll explain everything."

2:10pm

Dena noticed that her mother staring down at her hand again.

"Mom, what's wrong?"

"What? Oh, nothing. Do you know if either of the restrooms is available?"

They sat at a table in the café with a clear view of the two restrooms. If either of the people who had gone into them earlier had come out, her mother would know it.

"You're not going to wash your hands again, are you?" Dena asked. "That'll be like the twentieth time. Obsessive-compulsives don't wash their hands that much."

Her mother leaned forward over the table, lowering her voice. "I touched him, remember? I put my hand on his forehead to see if he had a temperature."

"Mom, there's nothing wrong with Dad."

"I know that," her mother said, though she looked like she knew nothing of the sort. "But I was just thinking . . . "

"Yes?" Dena prompted when her mother didn't go on.

"I should go over to the corner with your father."

"Even Dad shouldn't be stuck over there."

Her mother took a deep breath and composed herself, and Dena saw the anxiety melting from her mother's expression as if by magic. This was the woman Dena had known her whole life, calm and cool and always on top of everything. Idly, Dena found herself wondering if this had always been an act, a mask her mother put on to face her daughter and the world at large.

"This entire thing might be crazy," her mother said, "but the truth is we have no idea what this rain is, so precautions aren't a bad idea. We don't have to be so zealously gung-ho about it like that bald mother—um, fellow. But there is merit in the notion of a quarantine. And though indirectly, I have been exposed in a skin-to-skin contact sort of way. The responsible thing for me to do is to go sequester myself off with your father."

"Well, if you're going then I'm going, too," Dena said.

Her mother's mask cracked, letting through a glimpse of fear. "No. There's no need for you to do that because you haven't had direct physical contact with either me or your father since the rain started."

"Mom, I don't want to stay over here by myself with these people. I don't know any of them."

"It's not like we're going to be a million miles away," her mother said, attempting a light tone. She obviously wanted to don the mask of control again, but it was slightly askew and Dena could see her mother's true face beneath. "We'll be right around the corner."

Dena felt hot tears slipping down her cheeks to dribble off her chin. "Mom, please."

"Sweetheart, you're practically a grown woman. I know we don't always treat you like that, but you should know that your father and I see the woman you are blossoming into and we're incredibly proud of you. You're strong, determined, confident, and smart."

"Stop it," Dena said. "You're making this sound like goodbye."

"Actually, this is part of the speech I've been preparing for the day you go off for your first day of college, but events have led me to deliver it a bit prematurely."

Despite her continued tears, Dena found herself giggling. "You're telling me that you've actually prepared a speech to give for my first day of college?"

"Don't poke fun at my parenting techniques. I also pre-prepared the speech I gave you when you got your period, and I've already started on a speech for your wedding day. Big moments can be overwhelming; if you don't do some prep work, you just end up babbling."

Dena felt overcome with a warmth that enveloped her like a heated blanket. "Mom, I love you. I mean, I really love you."

"I know, and I love you too. That's why I'm doing this."

"Okay, but if you won't let me go with you then I'm moving up to the front of the store to be close by."

Her mother nodded and smiled. "Fine, except . . . not too close, promise?"

2:15pm

Tony couldn't concentrate on work.

After the incident with Dr. Argentine and the kid from the café, Tony had hung around up front for a while, talking with his husband. But after a few minutes, Vincent had insisted again that Tony return to work. Vincent was acting strangely, sort of uneasy and cagey, but that was to be expected considering the strange state of affairs.

Only, if Tony were completely honest with himself, Vincent had been acting strangely for quite a while now. Nothing major or overt, but not quite himself either. He had become a bit distant, easily distracted, and their lovemaking had become more perfunctory, more a chore than an act of passion.

That's natural, he told himself for the hundredth time. *You've been together five years; things are bound to be less exciting than they were in the beginning. Relationships are cyclical, with natural waxing and waning. Doesn't mean there's anything wrong.*

Tony cursed softly when he realized he'd just taped up a box without putting the ordered items inside. With everything happening right now, in the world at large and personally with his husband, it was insane that he was even attempting to continue working as if things were normal. Under the circumstances, Pamela would understand if he wanted to go ahead and clock out. He should go be with Vincent.

Tony turned away from his work station and let out a startled yelp when he found Yolanda standing in the doorway that separated the back area from the main store.

"We shouldn't let them stay in here with us, don't you think?" she said.

Tony noted that the young woman looked physically ill, her complexion ashy and her hands trembling as she kneaded them together.

"What are you talking about?" Tony asked, though he felt certain he knew exactly what she was talking about.

"The people who were out in the rain. They shouldn't be in here with us."

"You do realize that my husband is one of those *people*, right?"

"Hey, I'm not saying this is their fault or anything," she said. "It's like people who get AIDS. Doesn't mean they're bad or dirty, but it does make them dangerous."

Having come of age during the height of the AIDS epidemic, remembering when it was originally referred to as 'gay cancer', Tony bristled at her comparison. "Look, Yolanda, this isn't anything like AIDS. As far as we know, there's absolutely nothing in the rain that can make anyone sick."

"A bunch of high school kids in Long Island are sick now."

This news hit Tony like a slap to the face. "What?"

"It was just on the TV," Yolanda said. "They got caught out in the rain during lunch, hanging out in the quad. Now they're all sick. First the old guy, now these kids."

"Are any of the kids dead?"

"Not yet, but it's only a matter of time."

Tony stepped toward Yolanda, walking slowly as if approaching an unfamiliar dog that might either present its head to be petted or bite your hand off. "Did they say on the news that they were sure it was the rain that made them sick?"

Yolanda shook her head. "No, but what else could it be? I really think we shouldn't have anyone who got rained on in the store with us."

"I gotta agree," Jessica said, coming out of her office. "It's not safe."

Tony couldn't say he was surprised that Jessica held this opinion. Although he'd only known her a short while, she had already proven herself to be one of the biggest germophobes he'd ever met. If someone so much as borrowed a pen from her desk, she would Lysol her entire office and sanitize her hands so vigorously it seemed she wanted to rub her own fingerprints off. During cold and flu season, whether anyone in the store was sick or not, she routinely wore one of those face masks like doctors and nurses wear to work. He was surprised she wasn't wearing one now.

"They're all quarantined away by school supplies," Tony said.

Yolanda shook her head again. "Not good enough. We're still breathing the same air as them. That's not exactly a quarantine."

"Then what are you suggesting? That we just toss them all outside in the rain?"

"They can go next door to the Malerman Center," Jessica said. "They have that big lobby, more than enough room for them."

"Why don't you go put on one of your masks, Jessica?" Tony asked with more than a little snark.

Jessica shifted uncomfortably. "I'm out. I have some extras in my car, but . . . well, you know."

"Tony," Yolanda said, "I know you can't see this thing clearly because your husband is involved, but the smartest thing to do is to get them out of here."

"And you could always go with him," Jessica suggested.

Tony fixed the older woman with a heated glare. "Maybe you should be the one to join them. I mean, didn't you mop all that stuff up off the floor in the café?"

"Yeah, but I didn't get any of it on me."

"How can we be sure?" Yolanda said.

Tony felt a sinking in the pit of his stomach. He hadn't been serious, only wanted to say something to get under Jessica's skin, but Yolanda seemed to think it was a perfectly rational idea. Paranoia was beginning to run rampant.

"Guys, please, let's try to keep our heads," Tony said, fearing it was already a lost cause.

2:20pm

Pamela continued to man the café, even though at this point no one was really buying anything. She stood behind the counter, trying to block out the chatter of the customers (or were they really refugees at this point?), the drone of the news anchors on the television who kept talking without really saying anything new, and the steady drumming of the rain. That damn mystifying rain. She had no luck blocking out any of that, however. If anything, the sounds only amplified as if the store had become an echo chamber, creating a cacophony that reverberated inside her head, making it impossible for her to think. And she really needed to think right now.

A little while ago, she had left her post long enough to take a couple of towels and bottled waters over to Charlie and Dr. Argentine. She hadn't handed the items directly to the two men, instead sitting them down on the floor and stepping back. As if she were convinced that those who had been exposed to the rain were in fact contaminated.

But wasn't she convinced? Deep down where the ugly truth lived and thrived, didn't she believe they were contaminated?

From her vantage point, she could glance over to the corner with the school supplies and watch over the ones she had come to think of as The Exiled. What had started as seven had grown to ten. The addition of Charlie and Dr. Argentine had brought it up to nine, but then a few minutes ago a woman had joined them to be with her husband. Since Charlie and the professor were huddled together, almost everyone in that area was paired off. Everyone except Tony's husband and a female student.

She hated to admit it, but Pamela felt somehow safer with them over there . . . and yet not safe enough. The fact that she could still see them made her nervous.

Stop it, you're being ridiculous! You can't give in to the kind of mass hysteria Baldy is trying to spread. That isn't going to do anyone any good.

Tearing her eyes away from The Exiled, Pamela spotted Tony headed her way, his expression suggesting even more problems. He bypassed the counter and jerked his head to the side, indicating he wanted her to follow. The two of them met up in the storeroom.

"What is it?" she asked, a knot of dread forming in her stomach like a stone.

"I think you need to go talk to Yolanda and Jessica. They're starting to get a little addle-brained."

"You mean more so than usual?" Pamela said, the joke falling flat even to her own ears.

"I'm serious. They're talking about making the people who were out in the rain leave the store."

Pamela let out a small gasp. Tony no doubt thought she was shocked her employees would be saying something like that, but her surprise actually came from the fact that she had just been thinking damn near the same thing.

"The loud mouth bald guy is already whipping people up into a frenzy," Tony went on. "He seems to be getting a lot more people to listen to him. Reminds me a little too much of that crazy religious lady in *The Mist*."

"What's *The Mist*?"

"Never mind," Tony said. "The point is, we need to squash this before it becomes something dangerous."

"What do you think, that people will drag The Ex— I mean, the ones who were in the rain to the doors and toss them out?"

"Do I think they'll drag them out? No, because no one wants to touch them. But this kind of talk almost always leads to action of some type if left unchecked."

Pamela glanced over at The Exiled again, and this time she forced herself to look beyond her fear and to see the people. Real people, some of whom she knew. The old couple held each other, whispering softly to one another. The lone female student talked on her cell phone, and she seemed to be crying. Dr. Argentine had an arm thrown around Charlie. The young couple held hands. The couple where the wife had recently joined her husband were not touching but they stood close to one another; their daughter hovered not far from the unofficial quarantine area. Tony's husband pecked at his phone screen, apparently texting someone.

Tapping into her natural empathy, Pamela put herself in their place. As afraid as everyone was of them, imagine how afraid they must be themselves. She felt ashamed for wishing earlier that they were not in the store.

She turned back to tell Tony that she would go talk to Yolanda and Jessica, try to calm them down, but before she could speak a commotion arose from out in the store. Pamela and Tony exchanged a tense look, then ran out of the storeroom, Pamela in the lead.

In the café, people were gathering around the TV. *Sweet Jesus*, Pamela thought, *what else can possibly go wrong?*

But as she heard what the anchorwoman was saying, she discovered that finally there was some good news being delivered.

"To repeat for those just joining us, it has been confirmed that neither the previously reported death nor sickness of the high school students was actually a result of the rain. Orlando Granger from Phoenix, Arizona, passed away from cardiac arrest, and the students from Long Island City High School that fell ill were the victims of food poisoning resulting from some undercooked chicken."

Many of the people watching began to laugh and cheer, Pamela among them. Relief coursed through her, leaving her shaky on her feet. "Thank God," she said, over and over. "Thank you, God."

"Celebration may be a bit premature," said Baldy, his voice rising above the din.

"But they said that the rain didn't kill anyone or make anyone sick," said the post office worker.

Baldy laughed. "That's not what they said at all. They said the rain didn't cause that one guy to die or make that particular group of kids sick. They didn't say the rain was harmless. They still don't know what it is or what direct contact with it could do to a person. The jury is still out on that. So if you're entertaining the idea of letting those people over in the corner mingle with us, I'd give that some serious thought. They could still very well be dangerous, and we've been told nothing from anyone in authority to make us think otherwise."

Pamela scanned the group, and she could see the worry and fear returning to their faces. And she could feel tension returning to her own body.

Fuck, is this never going to end?

Excerpt from *The Day the Rains Came: An Annotated Timeline of the Deluge*

IT HAS TO be noted that the mainstream media holds some culpability in much of the panic that ensued around the globe. The sensationalistic nature of news programs vying for higher ratings than competitors led them to report events that should not have been reported until further information or corroboration was achieved. Once news began to spread on social media about the death of Orlando Granger and the illness of the Long Island City High School students, responsible media would have held off reporting about these incidents until they had evidence that these events were directly connected to the Deluge. However, in a race to be the first to report any scrap of information, no matter how tenuous, such caution was neglected. Yes, it is true that these reports largely included caveats that no one had definitively made a connection between the death/sickness and the rain, but by reporting them at all in conjunction with stories about the Deluge, a correlation was suggested that took root in the minds of people throughout the world.

By the time it was proven that the death of Granger and the illness of the high school students were not caused by the rain, the damage had been done and suspicion and paranoia were not so easily disarmed. In fact, some news organizations (FOX News being chief among them) continued to urge people to take extreme caution. That in and of itself is not bad advice, but the rhetoric became vitriolic as it suggested anyone exposed to the rain be removed from the company of 'the clean'. Even the President of the United States, who had previously downplayed the Deluge, switched gears and began talking about needing to draw a firm line between 'the clean' and 'the soiled', as he put it in a televised press conference.

2:40pm

LISA CHECKED THE cell screen and saw that her battery was nearly dead. Not altogether surprising; she hadn't charged it since sometime the day before yesterday, and she'd been on the phone with her father since this whole mess had started.

"Daddy, I'm scared," she said softly into the phone. She had isolated herself from the others that had been isolated here in the corner, a quarantine within quarantine. She sat on a wide windowsill next to a wire basket full of stuffed knights.

"Baby, I wish like hell I could be there with you, but don't be scared. No one has found anything harmful in the rain."

A *yet* hung unsaid, but Lisa didn't comment on it. Instead she said, "Tell that to the people here in the store with me. They still have us shoved off away from everyone else."

"But they're not forcing you, right?"

"Well, no. I mean, we're here voluntarily, but if one

of us decided we didn't want to stay over here anymore, I don't know what might happen."

"Just keep your head down. I'm sure this will be cleared up soon and we can get back to normal."

Empty promises, Lisa knew, but somehow when they came from her father they didn't seem quite so hollow. She found reassurance even in false hope, as long as his voice was the one delivering it.

"You know," she said, "if I run out to my car, I could be home in a little less than four hours."

"Don't even think about it."

"Why not? I can take one of the umbrellas from the store, and I've already been covered in the globs once. If it is going to do any damage, it's probably already done it by now."

"Lisa," her father said, and his use of her name and his tone told her he was about to go into lecture mode, "listen to me. I want you to stay put until this is over. I don't want you out on the roads right now. Please, for your old man's peace of mind, stay where you are. Promise me."

Lisa heaved a sigh. "Okay, I promise. But if these kooks in here get any kookier, I'm going to have to risk it."

"In the meantime, I'll stay on the line with you."

"Yeah, well, that reminds me, I need to do something right fast."

She got up from the windowsill and walked over to the electronics area of the school supplies, locating the appropriate phone charger. Not worrying about paying for it, she ripped into the package and returned to the window where she'd spotted an outlet beneath the basket full of knights.

~~~

2:55pm

Sitting on the floor with his back against a display case, Charlie thought he might start crying again, but with a concerted effort, he sucked it up and held it back. He'd been crying a lot since he got into the store. First he almost choked to death on a wad of bubblegum out front, then he got inside to find out that the entire world had gone mad. Almost made him wish he'd choked after all.

That wasn't true, of course, but things were pretty frightening. The only thing keeping him together was having Dr. Argentine nearby.

As if knowing Charlie was thinking about him, Dr. Argentine put a hand on Charlie's shoulder and squeezed. "Doing okay?"

"As okay as can be expected."

"Maybe you should try to eat something."

Earlier, the new shipping and receiving guy had brought over a tray full of sandwiches and pastries for the group in the corner. He lingered still, talking to a guy Charlie thought must be his husband. Dr. Argentine seemed awfully interested in them, and an odd part of Charlie felt jealous not to have the professor's full attention.

Funny thing was that Charlie had taken Freshman English Comp under Dr. Argentine last year and had paid the man almost no attention. He was like the wallpaper, or window treatments, a part of the room that just blended into the background and you noticed without noticing. Yet suddenly he felt like the most
~~~

important person in the world to Charlie. Of course, he realized this was mostly because the professor had saved Charlie's life, risking himself to run out into the rain, do the Heimlich, and pull him into the store. Also, in an uncertain time, he was the closest thing Charlie had to a parental figure.

"I'm not hungry," Charlie said, leaning to the side until his shoulder met Dr. Argentine's.

The professor shifted as if his position on the floor was uncomfortable, crossing his legs. "Still no luck in remembering either of your parents' numbers?"

Charlie shook his head. He was definitely a member of the digital generation. His family hadn't had a landline phone since Charlie was in diapers, but despite his parents each having had the same cell phones for years, Charlie didn't know the numbers by heart. Why did he need to when all he had to do was pick them out of the directory on his own phone?

Only now that he didn't have his phone with him, he had no way of calling them. They had probably called his own cell a thousand times by now and must be worried sick not being able to get in touch with him.

"If you know either of their emails, you can use my phone to send a message."

Charlie shook his head. He'd never emailed his parents in his life. Who emailed when you could text?

"Do either of them have social media accounts?"

"No, they think that stuff is frivolous. My mom once started an Instagram but after she only posted two pictures of our cat over the course of a year, she deleted it."

Dr. Argentine laughed. "Us old-timers don't always acclimate well to the newest technologies."

"You're not old," Charlie said. "You're . . . *distinguished.*"

"That's just a polite word for old."

"Well, I didn't mean it that way."

Dr. Argentine squeezed his shoulder again, then the professor's eyes once more strayed to where the shipping and receiving guy and his husband stood. They seemed to be having a rather heated discussion, and finally the shipping and receiving guy turned around and walked back toward the café.

"Excuse me for a minute, Charlie," Dr. Argentine said. Without waiting for any kind of a response, the professor pushed up to his feet and left Charlie alone, walking over to the shipping and receiving guy's husband.

Although Dr. Argentine was only a few feet away, Charlie felt absurdly abandoned. He lowered his head and allowed himself to cry again.

2:57pm

Vincent needed to piss. It wasn't a slight urge, but an actual biological *need*. As he watched Tony traipsing off to the café, Vincent felt an anger kindling inside of himself. First a lit match, but then the match lit a branch, and before he knew it there was a forest fire raging inside.

"I noticed you stopped texting when Tony came over," said a familiar voice to his left.

Vincent groaned and spoke to the professor without looking at him. "Are you being paid to harass me, Argentine? Because it seems like you've made it your full-time job or something."

"I'm just observant, is all. I noticed when your husband isn't around, you're texting up a storm, but the second he came over with the food, you turned your phone off and tucked it away. Kind of suspicious behavior, seems to me."

"Or maybe," Vincent said, turning to glare at Dr. Argentine, "when my husband is around I'm respectful enough to give him my undivided attention."

"Somehow I think the attention you give him is anything but *undivided*. You can play dumb all you want, but we both know you're the guy I chatted with on the hook-up site. I guess the only real question is, are you the type who goes on there because you get off on the thrill of playing with the idea of hooking up, or do you actually hook up with other men?"

The only desire Vincent had at the moment greater than the one to relieve his bladder was to punch that self-righteous look off the professor's smug face. Of course, he recognized that if life were a movie, Dr. Argentine would be the hero clearly on the moral high ground, and Vincent the slimy villain deserving of comeuppance—but life was never as straight-forward and black-and-white as the movies. Hollywood tended to avoid the complexities of moral gray areas.

"Listen, you sonofabitch," Vincent said, his voice low and heated. "I don't know you, I don't want to know you, and what goes on in my marriage is none of your goddamn business."

The smugness didn't crack one bit. "You may be right, but Tony seems like a truly great guy and I don't like the idea of someone who supposedly loves him taking advantage of him."

The proverbial lightbulb flared in Vincent's head,

and he thought he suddenly understood the man in front of him completely. "I see. So that's your angle, huh? Got the hots for my hubby, so if you could get me out of the picture maybe you'd stand a chance. Let me assure you, even if Tony was as single as they come, you wouldn't stand a chance."

For the first time, Dr. Argentine seemed flustered and at a loss for words, suggesting that Vincent had hit the bullseye. "I don't . . . I mean to say . . . my interest in Tony is only as a concerned friend."

"Friend? I get the impression Tony barely knows who you are. Why don't you go back to your barely-legal jailbait over there? Maybe he's still young and impressionable enough for you to get in his pants."

"That's absurd and nasty," Dr. Argentine said, but the color that came into his cheeks told Vincent that he'd scored another direct hit. "I can't imagine what Tony sees in someone so obviously morally bankrupt."

"Just fuck off, will you?"

The professor did leave, returning to the young man he'd pulled in out of the rain. Another heroic act that would make him the one movie audiences would cheer for.

The last thing he'd said to Vincent really stung. Had Vincent become morally bankrupt? He used to think of himself as a decent guy—not Mother Teresa with a penis (though some stories suggested the old nun had really been quite the bitch), but reasonably ethical. Then he'd started screwing around, which seemed to have opened some door to greater and greater depravity. At one point in his life, he never would have spoken to anyone the way he'd spoken to Dr. Argentine. He knew all the vitriol had less to do with the professor himself and more to do with the fact that the professor recognized a truth about Vincent that Vincent didn't want to face.

He began to shuffle from foot to foot, doing what his mother had called the 'pee dance' when he was little. He glanced over at the café to see Tony talking animatedly with the manager and that trouble-making bald fucker.

This was simply humiliating. Yes, Vincent had agreed to this isolation bullshit, but he'd never thought he'd have to get permission to cross the store to take a piss, like he was in kindergarten and had to get the teacher's say-so. Yet Tony had implored Vincent to wait a few moments so he could negotiate the situation. That was the exact word he'd used, *negotiate*. As if this were a terrorist making demands and not a man needing to perform a basic biological function.

"Screw this," Vincent said and started across the store, breaking the self-imposed quarantine.

3:00pm

Pamela's headache had gone from pounding to splitting to downright apocalyptic.

In front of her, Tony and Baldy (*I really should ask his name*, she thought vaguely) argued, their voices increasing in volume.

"Stop it!" she shouted, and they both instantly quieted. Turning to Baldy, she continued, "What exactly do you expect them to do? Just pull down their pants and do their business right on the floor by the binders and notebooks?"

He crossed his arms above his expanding gut, expression resolute. "I don't want them over here. Period."

"That doesn't answer my question about what you expect them to do when they need to go to the bathroom. The only two bathrooms in the store are over here by the café."

"That's not my—" Baldy's words cut off abruptly as his eyes switched to something behind Pamela. Suddenly his face scrunched up and he screamed, "What the fuck are you doing? Get the hell back over where you belong!"

Pamela turned to see Tony's husband approaching them. He held his hands up and slowed his step, but he didn't stop.

"I don't want any trouble," Vincent said. "I just need to use the bathroom, that's all."

Baldy sneered. "Why don't we send a mop bucket over to your side of the store?"

Vincent's hands dropped, any signs of conciliation dropping as well. "Listen, Mr. Clean, I don't know what makes you think you have any say in my comings and goings."

"The name is Langdon, and I'm just trying to keep everyone here safe from you people."

"I've heard that before from people more frightening than you. Like Anita Bryant."

Baldy (even though she now knew his name, she couldn't imagine thinking of him as anything but 'Baldy') looked confused. He opened his mouth for another retort, and Pamela knew she had to put a stop to this.

"Pause!" she said sharply. She then turned to

Vincent and softened her voice. “Of course you can use the bathroom. I do ask that you use the one on the left, okay?”

Vincent nodded. “Segregated bathrooms? How very separate-but-equal, but if it makes you feel better, fine.”

“Wait just a damn minute,” Baldy started in.

“If you don’t like it, I don’t care,” Pamela said to him. “This is *my* store. If you are so worried about it, you can go set up shop by the caps.”

Baldy glared at her like he wanted to crush her skull with the power of his mind, but he kept his mouth shut and began to back away while Vincent walked by, turning the corner into the short hallway that led to the bathrooms. Pamela watched him, ensuring that he did in fact go into the one on the left.

She had to admit, despite everything happening, a part of her indulged in a feeling of pride. She had always worried that her managerial style was too loose, too lax, and that while her employees liked her, she didn’t have the appropriate demeanor to really get people to do what she wanted. Yet here she was, being decisive and assertive and people were listening to her.

“You’re going to get us all killed,” Baldy said, keeping his voice low and staying back, as if afraid to even step into the general area where Vincent had walked.

“Stop with the melodramatic bullshit,” Tony said. “It’s been like two and a half hours since it started raining and no one is sick.”

“Not yet, no, but we have no idea how long of an incubation period this thing has.”

“What *thing*?” Pamela said. She still had her own

fears, her own misgivings, but she refused to let them turn her into an irrational person acting out of panic. "As far as we know, there is no *thing*."

Baldy pointed toward the windows. "Then what exactly is that shit raining down outside?"

"I have no idea, and neither do you."

"So they could still be dangerous," said a new voice behind Pamela.

Jessica, standing just outside the café area. Pamela was surprised the woman had dared scurry outside her office in the back.

"Look," Pamela said, rubbing at her temples again, "we'll have the ones who've had direct contact with the rain use the restroom on the left, and the rest of us will use the one on the right. I can't very well ask them to all sit over there and hold it, or go in their pants."

"They shouldn't be in the store at all."

Tony rolled his eyes and threw up his hands. "Please don't start that again."

"The Malerman Center lobby has its own restrooms, water fountains, snack machines," Jessica continued unabated. "I think the smart thing would be to move them over there."

Baldy's face lit up with a rapturous fire. "Now here's a woman who's making some sense."

"Jessica," Pamela said, "go back to your office and stop stirring the pot."

"It's not a bad idea," said the post office worker. "Not like we'd be sending them to the electric chair or anything. Just next door."

Other voices began to join in, the idea of making The Exiled migrate to the Malerman Center taking root and gaining steam in only a matter of seconds.

The voices quieted when Vincent came back down the hall from the restrooms. Everyone watched him in silence.

"What's going on?" he asked Tony.

"People being idiots," Tony said. "Come on, let's go."

"First, let's grab some chairs so we can have some places to sit over there."

Tony handed over four chairs to his husband, which he carried back-to-back, two in each hand. Tony took four more and they returned to school supplies.

"I think we should take a vote," Baldy said when they were gone.

"And do the ones over in school supplies get a vote as well?" Pamela asked.

Baldy smiled. "Why not? There are more of us than them anyway."

Jesus, Pamela thought. *There goes my feeling of finally being in charge.*

3:10pm

Eugene was worried about his wife. She had gone quite pale, and he noticed her hands were shaking.

"Helen, come sit down."

He helped her into one of the café chairs that the gay couple had brought back. Eugene took a seat next to her. Not the most comfortable chairs in the world, but it beat the floor. At their age, if Eugene and Helen hunkered down on the floor, it would probably take a crane to get them back up again.

"Are you okay?" he asked, realizing what a stupid question that was.

Helen tried on a smile, though the result was far from convincing, and patted the hand he put on her knee. "I guess what started off as a good day is taking a turn."

"Are you in pain?"

She nodded, closing her eyes as her face twisted in a grimace.

"Your pills?"

"Left them in the car like a ninny."

Eugene took his free hand and used it to cover Helen's hand, which in turn covered Eugene's hand resting on her knee. He hated seeing his wife in pain. He knew he could in no way truly understand the depth of her suffering, but he suffered in sympathy.

He tried not to linger on thoughts of what life would be like when Helen was gone. The two had been married for more years than most of the other people in this store had been alive. They'd met when they were in their early twenties, which meant Helen had been a part of his life for more years than she had not. Facing his remaining years without her by his side was almost too much for him to bear. He would have preferred to be the one to go first. Selfish, as it would leave Helen to deal with the loneliness and uncertainty that now waited for him, but he couldn't deny sometimes he felt that way.

"All things considered," Helen said, "maybe we should have stayed home today."

A surprised laugh sputtered from Eugene's lips, and Helen laughed as well, then grimaced again. She also clutched at her stomach.

"Helen, is there anything I can do for you?"

"Just be here with me, that's all."

"I'm not going anywhere."

Helen took a few deep breaths, then the tightness in her face softened somewhat. "I'm feeling a little nauseated," she said.

"Do you need me to help you to the restroom?"

She shook her head. "I think I'll be okay. For now, at least."

Eugene had never felt as helpless as he did in the face of the disease that ravaged his beloved wife. She leaned forward again, her mouth stretching into a thin line, as another pain spasm gripped her, and the hand sandwiched between his own trembled like a spider in the grips of a seizure.

"You need your pills," he said, more to himself than to his wife.

"If wishes were horses," she said with a weak smile.

Eugene felt himself overwhelmed with not just love for his wife but also intense admiration. In the face of the cancer, she displayed more bravery than he'd ever seen, even when serving in the army during World War II. Perhaps it was his time to show some bravery for her sake.

Glancing around to make sure no one was in earshot, he leaned closer to his wife and said, "I'll be right back."

"Where are you going? Bathroom?"

"No, I'm going to get your pills."

Helen's eyes widened, and she started to speak, but Eugene put a finger to her lips to silence her.

"You need your pills, and I'm going to get them. That's all there is to it."

"But the rain."

"What about it? We don't know there's anything harmful in it, and if there is, well . . . "

He didn't finish that sentence. He didn't need to.

"They won't like it," Helen said, gesturing toward the café.

"I don't plan to ask their permission. I'm already over here in quarantine anyway. I'm going to try to slip out without anyone seeing me. I promise I won't be long."

Helen put a hand on the back of his head and kissed him. A kiss like they hadn't shared in many years, one of those passionate kisses from the early years of their courtship.

"I love you, Eugene Terrance McArthur."

"And I love you, Helen Marie Simmons McArthur."

After another quick kiss, Eugene stood and headed toward the front of the store. He tried not to rush, tried not to attract attention from anyone else. Of course, he suspected one never looked more conspicuous than when trying to act casual.

Still, everyone seemed preoccupied in their own private worlds, which worked in his favor. He made it all the way to the front without anyone seeming to notice him. At the doors, he paused, looking out at the rain. Had it slackened a bit? He couldn't be sure, but it certainly hadn't stopped. He would have liked an umbrella at least, but he wasn't going anywhere near the café to grab one out of the display.

"Here goes nothing," he murmured then pushed open the door just enough to slip out.

3:15pm

Dena closed her eyes and released her breath in a

relieved sigh. She hadn't expected the vote to go her way.

When the manager had asked everyone in the store (except those segregated in the corner) to gather in the café, she hadn't wanted to stray too far from her parents, but she'd gone reluctantly. Then when she found out a vote was being taken on whether or not to make the ones in the corner actually leave the store, terror had seized her by the throat. She'd wanted to run back and tell her parents, but she didn't want to worry them if she didn't need to. And at first she hadn't believed that people would really vote to kick them out.

She'd argued against it, the store manager had argued against it, and the other store worker who she thought was married to one of the guys over there with her parents argued against it. However, theirs seemed to be the only dissenting voices, and Dena had started to worry.

As opposed to a show of hands, the manager had suggested a secret ballot. Everyone was handed a Post-It and instructed to write either 'Leave' or 'Stay' on it, then toss it into an empty Grande cup.

Dena had waited tensely while the votes were counted, expecting it to be three votes for 'Stay' and the rest 'Leave'.

However, when the votes were all counted, the tally stood at twelve 'Stay' and ten 'Leave'. Apparently there were more people of conscience here who simply didn't feel comfortable being vocal about it. A narrow victory, but a victory nonetheless.

"There you go," the manager said, though her expression suggested some conflicting feelings about the result. She addressed the bald sonofabitch who seemed to be the start of all this trouble. "The people have spoken."

The bald guy said nothing at first, actually took all the Post-Its and recounted them. Once, and then a second time for good measure.

"What is wrong with you people?" he said, turning three hundred and sixty degrees. "These people need to go."

"*These people* happen to be family to some of us," said the guy married to one of the segregated.

"Then you can go with them."

"Nobody is going anywhere," the manager said. "You wanted to vote, so we voted. Perfectly democratic."

The bald guy looked like he wanted to spit nails, an expression Dena had never understood until now. This guy looked like he'd like to spit a railroad-spike-sized nail into the forehead of everyone in the café. "You idiots are putting us all in danger."

"Oh, would you just shut the fuck up!" Dena growled, surprising even herself. Normally if her parents heard her dropping the F-bomb, there would be hell to pay. However, in this instance she suspected they would have cheered her on.

The bald guy stared at her, all of his ire seeming to concentrate and zero in on her like a laser beam. "Listen, little girl, your parents should have taught you better than to speak to your elders like that."

"My parents, who are two of the people you seem to want to kick out of here, taught me to speak up against ignorant blowhards. And I'd say you definitely qualify."

"Who are you calling ignorant, little girl?"

Dena normally considered herself somewhat of a meek person. Not shy exactly, and not cowardly, but she tended to avoid conflict and confrontation if at all possible. However, she was discovering an unexplored well of ferociousness that she hadn't even suspected existed within her.

"I'm calling you ignorant, you little piss-ant. My dad isn't sick. My mother, who is only over there to keep him company, isn't sick. In fact, not a single soul over there is sick. So what you need to do is shut your—"

Dena was interrupted by a shrill scream. Not from anyone in the café. The scream came from somewhere over near the school supplies.

3:17pm

Lisa could hear her father shouting through the phone, asking what was wrong, but she'd let the hand holding her cell drop to her side when she screamed. Near her, the old woman had slipped out of her chair, onto her hands and knees, and threw up on the carpet. The woman's husband was there the last time Lisa had looked that way, but now he was nowhere to be seen.

The other people stuck here in this No Man's Land gathered around, asking the woman if she was okay, but no one dared touch her.

Lisa didn't want to get anywhere near her, and in fact started walking away, putting more distance between them. The woman was sick, clearly sick, which meant maybe the rain was toxic after all.

Of course, if that were true, Lisa herself was already exposed, already infected, so distancing herself from the old woman wasn't going to do her any good at this point.

She heard footsteps rushing up behind her and turned to find the rest of the store (the uninfected) running this way. They all stopped at a safe distance.

"What's going on?" the manager of the store asked.

Lisa pointed a shaking finger at the old woman. "There's something wrong with that lady."

The woman was using the chair to get back to her feet. "I'm okay," she said. "Just a little sick."

"No shit you're sick!" yelled the bald man. "What did I tell you all? It's starting. We have to get these people out of here!"

Excerpt from *The Day the Rains Came: An Annotated Timeline of the Deluge*

IT WOULD BE remiss of this author not to point out that the majority of people on the planet handled this situation with grace, dignity, compassion, and empathy. Despite panic and uncertainty, most people managed to retain their sense of humanity, charity, and generosity. This book will detail several stories of people going above and beyond to take care of each other in a time of crisis, such as the countless churches that opened their doors to the homeless or the teachers that used their own bodies to shield students from the rain.

However, it would also be remiss not to mention the instances where the better part of human nature did not prevail. The instances of people being locked out of their own homes by family members; rioting and looting; the people who were shot while seeking shelter.

Though these instances proved to be less common, what truly disturbs is how quickly otherwise civilized people turned to this type of behavior; law-abiding citizens devolving into lawlessness in such a brief span. The event itself lasted exactly three hours, starting at 12:23:15pm EST and ending at 3:23:15pm EST.

3:19pm

PAMELA FELT FROZEN. Everyone around her was yelling, she could feel things getting out of control, but she couldn't make herself speak, couldn't make herself act. Mainly because she didn't know what she wanted to say, what she wanted to do.

Only moments ago she had committed herself to rationality, to level-headedness, but seeing the old woman on her hands and knees, vomiting . . . all that fled away to be replaced with a primal, animal fear. Fear of corruption, of being tainted, of the *unclean*. She just wanted the woman—all of The Exiled—as far from her as possible.

Deep in her brain, a voice tried to speak up, to point out the woman's sickness may have nothing to do with the rain, that jumping to conclusions did no one any good, that this could be as coincidental as the heart attack and the food poisoning incidents. However, in the din it was easy to ignore that voice.

She realized an outside voice was shouting in her ear. Tony, next to her, shouting, "Pamela, do something!"

She opened her mouth, not sure how she was going to respond until the words fell from her lips. Almost without being aware of it, she repeated Baldy's sentiment nearly verbatim. "We need to move these people to the lobby next door."

Thomas tried to stand, but Charlie clung to him, arms locked around the professor's midsection like a vice. Thomas hated to admit it, but even in a situation such as this, his body responded to the young man's closeness and the physical contact. Thomas felt himself stiffen.

Even if things weren't so dire, he knew he shouldn't be feeling this way about a student. Yet Charlie was undeniable adorable, made even more so because the young man seemed totally unaware of the impact his baby face, curly hair, and smooth skin had on other people.

Shaking away the inappropriate lust, he extricated himself from Charlie, gripping the young man's shoulders and speaking directly into his face. "You stay here. I need to go talk some sense into these people before they turn into a mob."

"Like in *Frankenstein*," Charlie said, the corners of his mouth flickering.

"Yes, now you stay put."

Thomas started to rise, and then Charlie clasped his hand with a desperate ferocity. "You'll come back, right?"

"Of course. I won't leave you."

At first he didn't think Charlie was going to release his hand, but finally the boy let go and Thomas hurried over to the shouting group.

Vincent found himself flashing back to his youth, bullies on the school yard surrounding him, calling him 'pussy' and 'faggot' while pushing and shoving him. He knew the look and sound of dangerous group-think when it stood before him.

And while he had come a long way from that scrawny kid on the playground, gaining confidence and self-assurance to go with his increased muscle mass, he found himself afraid. Looking at the group, he recognized the signs in them. They were afraid themselves, but they had turned that fear into anger because anger came with a greater sense of control. But anger served no purpose if it didn't have a target at which to aim itself. A scapegoat was needed, a sacrificial lamb. Or, in this case, goats and lambs.

Right now it was just screaming and yelling, but this would inevitably lead to action. Vincent had no doubt they were going to make those who had come into contact with the rain leave the store. Even if they had to drag them out kicking and screaming.

Vincent met Tony's eyes, and his husband made a subtle move of the head to the left, then faded back to the rear of the group then around, disappearing behind a rack of backpacks. Slowly Vincent began to back up himself. Everyone on both sides was so totally invested in the shouting match that no one seemed to be paying him any attention as he met Tony on the other side of the backpacks.

Tony stood in front of a glass door, his work keys in hand. "This leads to the textbook room," he said in a whisper. "We only keep it open the first couple weeks of a new semester. I can take you through there and into the back."

As Tony turned and fumbled one of the keys into the lock, Vincent reached out and placed a firm hand against the door, holding it closed. He did this without thought, acting on instinct.

"What are you doing?" Tony said. "Pamela is on their side now. They are going to make you all leave."

Vincent nodded. "I know, and maybe we should."

"What?"

Vincent stared at his husband, and was overcome with such a massive tidal wave of love that it nearly buckled his knees. Raul was needy, constantly wanting Vincent to take care of him, but here Tony was, wanting to take care of Vincent. Always putting Vincent first. What the hell had Vincent been thinking, fucking around and daring to think he loved Raul? What a fool he'd been. That needed to end now; he needed to start putting Tony first.

"Fact is, we could be dangerous," Vincent said. "I don't want anything to happen to you, so I think we should leave."

Dena ran to her mother and threw herself into her arms.

"It's okay," her mother said as she squeezed her tight.

Okay? Nothing was okay. The world had gone crazy, and the people in this store even crazier.

"Please, let's just stop screaming," her dad was saying, raising his hands above his head, trying to get everyone's attention. "I'm sure we can work something out."

A woman stepped forward and spit in her dad's face. "Only thing to work out is if you're going to leave here willingly or by force."

Eugene made it back to the overhang, clutching the bottle of Helen's pain medication in his right hand. Even through the door, he could hear raised voices. He pushed his way in quickly.

During the brief moments he'd been gone, the entire store had converged over at the school supplies. He spotted his wife, bent over in her chair, clutching her stomach and shaking. He headed toward her.

A man spotted Eugene and let loose with an inarticulate scream, and suddenly everyone was looking at him.

"Another one," the bald guy shouted, pointing at him, reminding Eugene of the final shot in the 1970s version of *Invasion of the Body Snatchers*. "We need to get these people out of here before they kill us all!"

"Daddy, I think I screwed up big time," Lisa said into the phone.

"Baby, what's going on?" he answered, though she could barely hear him over all the raised voices around her. She wasn't sure she wanted to tell her father what was going on anyway, considering her culpability.

She hadn't meant for this to happen, but what had she expected? She had been the one to sound the alarm, to call the mob over, to rat out the old woman being sick. And now the barely controlled chaos in the store had spilled over, and she was afraid someone was going to get hurt.

And it would be all her fault.

Charlie pulled his knees up to his chest and placed his hands over his ears. He wished Dr. Argentine would come back. Call it security-blanket-syndrome, but he felt somehow safer with the man next to him.

Everyone was screaming, and Charlie found

himself flashing back to the day he'd come out to his parents during his sophomore year of high school. There had been a great deal of screaming then as well, and much like now, he'd worried he was going to get kicked out.

Eventually his parents had come around, and even if they weren't thrilled with the fact that their only son was a homosexual, they had made peace with it and seemed to accept him. Which was great, but a part of him would never quite get over the fact that their initial reaction had been anger and disappointment and screaming.

Charlie tried to make himself into a tight ball, willing himself to become invisible.

Tony tried to talk some sense into Vincent, but for some reason Vincent wouldn't listen. He seemed serious about leaving the store. Distantly, Tony found this curious as Vincent had never exactly been the throw-himself-on-the-grenade type of person. And now hardly felt like the time to develop a martyr complex.

Vincent was headed back around the rack of backpacks, and Tony reached out and grabbed his arm. "You don't have to—"

Vincent reacted as if he'd been grabbed by a giant slug. He jerked his arm away and his nose wrinkled in disgust. At first Tony felt stung, but then he realized the disgust wasn't aimed at him.

Vincent was disgusted with himself.

"You shouldn't touch me," he said. "I could be toxic for all you know. You're better off keeping your distance from me. Seriously."

Vincent spoke with such an intensity that for a moment Tony had the feeling that they were talking about more than this crazy rain. He shook the thought from his head and said, “We don’t know that for sure. We don’t know *anything* for sure.”

Vincent shrugged. ‘Better safe than sorry’ is a philosophy that never hurt anyone.”

Before Tony could respond, Vincent turned and walked away.

The group around Pamela had begun chanting, “Get them out! Get them out!” Over and over. More than a mantra. A promise. A threat. She saw Baldy, the post office worker, Jessica, Yolanda, and so many other faces twisted by fear and something that looked like hate. Spittle flying from their mouths. The look of cult members, of mindless zombies caught up in the grips of mania.

Part of her brain whispered that she should do something to stop them, but she couldn’t at the moment.

She was too busy chanting along with them.

Thomas tried using his lecture voice, the one he used in class to gain the students’ attention and respect. The voice that said he was an authority and should be listened to. This voice was lower than his normal voice; deeper, and more confident.

It usually worked in the classroom, but it wasn’t working here. He may as well have been invisible. In an odd way, this reminded him of how it felt the last time he tried going out to a gay club. An old man in a sea of 'twinks'. If that was a term the younger generations even used anymore. Thomas may as well have been acting out that old H.G. Wells novel as he passed ghost-like through the multitudes.

Right as he decided to give up and rejoin Charlie, he saw an old man who was covered in the slimy gunk from the rain trying to make his way through the crowd to the little quarantine corner. People were screaming at him, and the bald man reached over and pulled a heavy three-ring binder off a shelf and threw it at the old guy, hitting him in the side of the face. Thomas could see a gash open up at the man's temple, blood beginning to dribble down.

This has to stop! Someone has to do something!

Thomas looked around and zeroed in on the small checkout counter on this side of the store. It was unmanned except for the rush that came during the start of a new semester, and Thomas ran to it, jumping on top of the counter. He stomped his foot several times, like a bull about to charge, and he screamed in a way he never had before, with such force that his throat hurt from the strain. He knew he had to do something to truly get people's attention, so he screamed the most absurd sentence he could think of.

"PETER PARKER IS A SHIT-SHOVELING BITCH!"

Ridiculous as it was, this seemed to do the trick. The shouting in the store cut off like a needle being lifted from a record, and all eyes turned to him. For a moment, he found himself at a loss for words now that he had the stage.

Finally he cleared his throat, and recognizing how

silly this sounded following his previous outburst, he said, "We need to be sensible here."

3:20pm

Vincent stared at the silly professor standing up on the countertop like he thought he was Robin Williams in *Dead Poets Society. 'Oh Captain, my Captain!'*

And then yelling out gibberish like that. Had the man completely lost his mind or what?

Then again, Vincent had to admit the ploy got results. Everyone shut the hell up and started paying attention to the professor. Now if only the professor had something to actually *say*, which he obviously didn't.

But this provided an opportunity for Vincent to say what he needed to say.

"He's right, a little sense is needed," Vincent said, stepping forward. All eyes turned from the professor to him. "And my common sense tells me that Mr. Clean is right. We need to separate ourselves."

"What?" said the young man who'd stuck his hand out in the rain earlier, thus earning himself a spot with the other tainted.

Tony came up behind Vincent and said, "Please don't do this."

Vincent ignored them both and continued. "I feel fine. As far as any of us know, there's nothing harmful about the rain—"

"The old woman is sick," the bald fucker said.

The woman in question's husband had made his way to her, holding a hand to his bleeding head. "She has cancer," he said.

Mr. Clean smirked. “So you say. We just supposed to take your word for it?”

The old man held up an orange prescription bottle. “I’ve got her pain meds right here. Want me to call her doctor and get him to confirm for you?”

Vincent could sense control slipping away again, so he raised his voice and said, “If you would let me finish, I was going to say that even though we don’t know there’s anything harmful about the rain, it would still be prudent to err on the side of caution.”

No one spoke at first. Even the bald fucker seemed flabbergasted as if having Vincent agree with him made him reevaluate his whole position.

Into the silence, Vincent continued. “It’s just like with the Coronavirus a few years ago. We had to make some decisions that none of us wanted to make, but we did it for the greater good. For the sake of those we love. We need to make those hard decisions now as well.”

“Exactly,” the bald fucker yelled, though Vincent suspected he would have been the type during the Corona pandemic to protest lockdown and self-isolation.

“You’re not getting me out there,” said the male student who clearly didn’t feel like he belonged here, his girlfriend gripping his arm. “That’s nuts.”

“No, it’s not,” said the professor, clambering down off the counter. “I think in the interest of public safety, even if only as a measure of precaution, we should remove ourselves.”

“I agree,” said a man who stood with his wife and daughter.

"Dad, no," Dena cried. "Don't let that bald sonofabitch bully you into doing something stupid."

Her dad reached for her then retracted his arms, letting them fall by his side. "It's not stupid. It's actually smart. I'm not saying 'that bald sonofabitch', as you so eloquently put it, is smart, but we shouldn't be around the rest of you. At least not until we have a better handle on what's happening here."

"I'm not letting you go out there alone."

"Yes, you are!" her dad said, the sharpness of his voice surprising her. He had always been a gentle man—when she was in middle school, she had started to think of him as a wimp before maturity made her see how much strength it took for a man to show his sensitive side. He had never raised his voice to her in this way, not even the time she'd accidently driven her bike into the side of his car, leaving a pretty nasty dent and scratch. "You and your mother are going to stay here."

"No way!" the bald sonofabitch said. "Tangential contact may be just as bad; we don't know. I say every single person who has had contact with anyone caught out in the rain needs to go."

Pamela felt like she was waking up, or surfacing from underwater. More to the point, she felt like a spell had been broken.

This reminded her of the time in high school when she and some girlfriends had gone to see a traveling preacher because they thought it would be funny. He had been preaching against the evils of secular music and rock 'n' roll, that whole spiel. At first it had seemed ridiculous and laughable, but as the sermon wore on, she and her friends found themselves getting into it, and the things he said started to make sense. They had ended up running out to their cars, gathering up their CDs, and bringing them back into the auditorium to throw them on the stage along with many other people in attendance, ridding themselves of the 'wicked music'. Caught up in the furor and fever. Afterward, in the parking lot, Pamela and her friends found that fever fading, and Pamela gave voice to what she suspected they all were thinking: "Why in the hell did we do that?"

That was how she felt now. Had she just been chanting along with Baldy and his acolytes? Yes, she had, and she felt ashamed. Not so ashamed that she didn't still want The Exiled out of the store, but ashamed enough that she felt some parameters had to be set.

"Let's everyone pause for a second," she said. "If we are going to do this, we have to be reasonable. It should only be the ones who actually were in the rain."

Tony's husband spoke up again. "Okay, let's vote among those of us here in quarantine. Who all is willing to move next door?"

Tony watched in numbed silence as his husband raised his hand. Then Dr. Argentine, the man with the family, the old couple, Charlie from the café, the female student whose scream had called them all over here. The last holdout was the male student who at this point must truly be regretting sticking his hand out into the rain right after it started, but his girlfriend whispered softly to him, telling him she would go with him, and he finally raised his hand as well.

"So it's settled," Vincent said, turning to the bald fucker. "You can put your torches and pitchforks away. The monsters are going to go quietly."

Hearing the word 'monsters' made Tony realize what this situation reminded him of. That old *Twilight Zone* episode where the power goes off in a neighborhood and the residents become cut off from the rest of the town, and things quickly devolve into paranoia and accusation and eventually violence.

"Vincent, please," Tony started, but his husband didn't let him finish.

"You're staying here, Tony," Vincent said then reached out as if he were going to caress Tony's face, stilling his hand a few inches before making contact. "You deserve better than me. I'm not sure if you know that, but I know it."

Tony wasn't sure how to respond to this. And before he could, Vincent walked away.

Charlie clung to the professor's arm as they made their way slowly across the store toward the exit by the café, the closest to the Malerman Center next door. "Are you sure this is the right thing to do?"

Dr. Argentine glanced behind them to where the crowd was following those leaving at a distance, but forming a wall of flesh. He then offered Charlie a weak smile and said, "Honestly, I think we'll be safer out there than cooped up in here with these folks."

"Okay, then maybe we should go to my dorm room."

A blush crept into the professor's cheeks, and Charlie wasn't sure why.

Except that was a lie. He knew why, and if he were completely honest with himself, he had to admit he didn't mind. He found it rather flattering. Perhaps it was an aftereffect of the gratitude he felt for Dr. Argentine saving his life, but the sentiment was even reciprocated, at least a little.

"Oh, I don't know," Dr. Argentine stammered. "Maybe we should stick with the others."

Charlie gripped his arm even tighter, pulling the professor closer to him. "Please, I just want to go back to my room but I don't want to be alone. We can get showered, and my roommate is out but I think he probably has some jogging pants and sweatshirts that might fit you."

The professor hesitated a moment before answering. "Um, okay, sure."

3:21pm

At the café, Pamela skirted around The Exiled, getting in front of them. The Pied Piper leading the rats to the water. She had to admit, if anyone here were calling the shots it was Baldy, or maybe Tony's husband, but she needed to do something to assert herself, to put herself back in charge of things. Even if it was all just for show.

At the door, she paused with her hand outstretched. Though glass separated her from the rain, she felt herself recoiling inside. A primal, instinctual reaction; the reaction of early man encountering a poisonous snake or a saber-toothed tiger. The reaction of coming face-to-face with a force of nature stronger and more deadly than yourself.

How can I send these people out into this? she thought, immediately followed by, *They all grabbed umbrellas on the way over here. Besides, they've already been exposed. What more harm can it do?*

Of course, she didn't know. None of them knew, they were flying blind. The TV still played endless talking heads, sharing theories and conjecture but offering no firm answers, no real substantive information. Was sending The Exiled into further exile the right thing to do, the wrong thing? Did it matter?

Taking a deep breath, she grabbed the door handle and pulled it open. If she wanted to be seen as the leader then she had to start acting the part. She needed to be decisive; a woman of action. No room for internal debates, reservations, or indecision.

The Exiled hesitated for a moment, and she worried they would collectively change their minds. She wasn't sure what would happen if that were to occur.

But then Tony's husband, in the lead, turned and told Tony he loved him before popping his umbrella and dashing out into the rain, making a beeline for the Malerman Center. The door was only a few feet away, but it suddenly seemed like miles to Pamela.

The old couple went next, sharing one of the oversized maroon-and-white umbrellas. Then they all started filing out, heads down and an overwhelming sense of dread radiating off them like a scent. *Walking the plank posture,* she thought.

She noticed when Dr. Argentine and Charlie left, both huddled together under a single umbrella, they didn't run toward Malerman—instead cutting to the left as if heading toward the dorms.

What do I care, as long as they are out of here and away from me?

Pamela felt ashamed of such a thought. Dr. Argentine could be a bit of a pompous ass sometimes but he was basically a decent guy, and Charlie was a sweetie. Still, didn't change her feelings.

The last of The Exiled to leave was the young male student and his girlfriend. At the doorway, the girl suddenly stopped. "I can't go through with it."

Her boyfriend glanced back at her. "What are you talking about? You're the one who said we should do this."

The girl locked eyes with Pamela. "She said that only the people who came into direct contact with the rain had to go. I didn't come into direct contact, so I don't have to go. Right, lady? Isn't that what you said?"

Caught off guard, Pamela could only nod.

"You said you'd come with me," the boy said, grabbing his girlfriend's arm. "That's the only reason I agreed to go along with this bullshit. You said you'd stay by my side."

The girl wrenched her arm loose and backed away from him, tears leaking down her cheeks. "I'm sorry, Nick. I can't, I just can't."

The boy let loose with a growl of frustration, pulling at his hair. "Then fuck this, and fuck all y'all. I'm not going out there, I'm staying put!"

"The hell you are!" Baldy shouted, stepping

forward while Pamela remained frozen, again showing himself to be the one truly in charge.

The boy folded his arms against his chest. "Who's gonna make me leave, geezer? You?"

Baldy smiled, an ugly slash across the lower part of his face, then held out his arms to indicate all those around him. "Looks like I've got an army here."

Though the boy's posture didn't change, this close Pamela could see a shift in his eyes. An uncertainty and fear dawning.

"Oh hell," Baldy said with a greasy laugh. "I don't need an army."

Moving more swiftly than Pamela would have thought possible, Baldy picked up one of the chairs at the tables nearest him and tossed it at the boy. Baldy's throw went low (by design or shoddy aim, she wasn't sure) and it struck the boy in the thighs. He stumbled back, through the door that Pamela still held open, then fell back onto his bottom.

Baldy rushed forward, roughly pushing Pamela aside, and shut the door, turning the lock. Speaking to no one in particular, he shouted, "Go lock the door at the front!"

Several people—including Jessica, Yolanda, and the post office worker—ran that way to obey their leader's order.

3:22pm

Vincent was already inside the Malerman Center, his umbrella discarded (it had done only marginal good anyway; he'd gotten coated all over again), holding the door open for the rest of his fellow outcasts when he saw the young male student fall backward out of the bookstore, landing hard on his rear end.

From this distance and at this angle, Vincent couldn't be sure what had happened, but the boy fell with such force, it seemed as if he had been pushed. Vincent waited to see the boy's girlfriend come out after him, but instead the door to the bookstore closed. The boy jumped back to his feet and launched himself at the door, beating on the glass.

Everyone else had made it inside Malerman. Except for the nosy professor and the kid who had become attached to his hip. They'd run off in the opposite direction. To find help, to screw, Vincent didn't know and didn't care.

He waited for the boy outside to get tired of beating at the door and go join the rest of them, but instead he turned and leaned his back against the glass, sliding down until he sat on the pavement again. He seemed to be crying.

"Oh for fuck's sake," Vincent said, then went back outside. He didn't bother with the umbrella this time; he was already covered in the slime. His guilt over cheating on Tony had him overcompensating with the selfless Good Samaritan bit. When he reached the boy, Vincent crouched down and said, "Come on, let's get inside."

"She didn't come with me, man," the boy said, the rain sliding down his face like snot. "She said she loved me, but she let them throw me out here by myself."

"Yeah, women. Can't live with 'em, can't . . . well, I don't know really have anything to follow that. How about we get in out of the rain?"

The boy didn't say anything, but when Vincent took his arm, he allowed himself to be lifted onto his feet. The two were halfway back to the Malerman Center when Vincent realized something was wrong. He wasn't sure what it was at first, but something was definitely wrong.

Only when a ray of sunlight glinted off the metal and glass of the Malerman's facade did he realize that what was *wrong* was that suddenly something was *right*.

It had stopped raining.

3:23pm

Thomas and Charlie were just outside the dorm building when the rain stopped.

They both skidded to a halt, and Thomas stared up at the sky, blinking as if not quite trusting his eyes. Or any of his senses, for that matter. A part of him had expected it to never stop raining, just a continued downpour like the biblical flood in Noah's time. Only this time God decided to cover the world in slime instead of water, which seemed a fitting metaphor somehow.

As he stared up at the sky, the clouds began to dissipate like smoke, allowing shafts of sunlight to filter through, as well as mosaic patches of blue.

"Is it over?" Charlie asked with the naked desperation of a child after viewing his first horror movie.

Thomas shook his head then realized he had lowered the umbrella let it drop to the ground. The phenomenon certainly appeared to be over, but he seemed to remember something about the incident in Washington in 1994; he thought it had rained the blobs a few more times after the initial downpour. "I don't know. Maybe I should get home."

Charlie grabbed his hand. "No, don't leave me. Let's just go to my room."

"I'm parked up by the auditorium. Now that the rain has stopped, the smart thing would be to get off campus."

"Please," Charlie said, refusing to let go of Thomas's hand. "Just come to my room with me. I'll call my parents right fast to let them know I'm okay and then we can shower . . . together, if you want."

At first Thomas was too gob-smacked to respond. He stammered a moment before saying, "You know I'm old enough to be your—"

Charlie silenced him with a kiss. A kiss full of fire and urgency, and Thomas felt his body respond. And they were pressed so closely together that he was sure Charlie could feel it as well. Both their lips were coated in the gunk, and he realized that people in the dorms could possibly see them through the windows, caught in this highly inappropriate act that could potentially cost him his job, yet none of that mattered in the moment.

Finally Charlie pulled back and said, "Come on."

This is wrong, I can't do this, Thomas thought, even as he followed Charlie into the dorm.

"Let me out," Tony said, standing before the group that blocked his way to the door. "What, are we prisoners in here now?"

The bald guy said, "I'm trying to keep us safe, whether you realize it or not."

Tony had watched through the smeared glass as Vincent came and retrieved the young student who had been knocked out of the store with the chair. The kid's girlfriend hadn't stopped crying, and Pamela was trying to comfort her. And now the rain had stopped.

"If he wants to leave, just let him leave," Jessica said. "As long as he understands he isn't coming back in."

"Why can't we all leave?" Yolanda asked. "It's not raining anymore."

Not anywhere, according to the news. The televisions had become nothing more than background noise these last few hours, but now Tony became aware of the reporters announcing that the rain had stopped everywhere, all at once. Unlike the gradual and escalating start to the rain, the end came abruptly for everyone.

"But that shit is still out there, covering everything," the bald guy said. "The ground, the trees, our cars. There's no way we can go out there without coming into contact with it. Best to wait it out a bit."

Most of the people left in the store murmured their agreement, and Tony was about to renew his argument to let him out when a loud racking cough exploded behind him.

Everyone turned to see Yolanda bent over with the force of her coughing, eyes squeezed shut. The cough had a rattling, liquid sound to it.

"Are you okay?" Jessica asked, stepping toward Yolanda.

But she stopped and let out a quiet gasp when

Yolanda straightened up and let her hand fall away from her mouth. Both her lips and fingers were tacky with blood.

3:24pm

When Pamela saw the blood, she instinctively moved toward Yolanda. The female student who had watched her boyfriend get thrown out of the store continued to cling to her, so she was dragged along.

"Stay back!" Baldy shouted, and Pamela stopped moving, annoyed that even she herself was listening to the man like he was the boss. "That girl has obviously been infected as well."

Yolanda stared down at her bloody fingers, and her entire body quivered. Pamela could see sweat beginning to run down her face in rivulets. "No, it can't be. I never went out in the rain."

"Then you must have touched someone who did," Baldy said. "It's the only explanation."

Yolanda began shaking her head no, and even though Pamela couldn't recall any time Yolanda had come anywhere near those who had been out in the rain, she could think of no other explanation. Then she thought of the girl who presently clung to her; her boyfriend had stuck his hand out in the rain. Had the girl perhaps held that very hand since then? It was at least possible.

She tried to extricate herself gently, but the girl didn't want to let go. Pamela ended up giving the girl a shove so that she bumped into a display of power bars, knocking several of them to the floor. The girl seemed to be sweating as well, and in fact, Pamela could feel droplets of perspiration dribbling down her own face.

"Get her out, get her out," the post office worker screeched, going to the door and twisting the lock to open it.

"Please, it's not—" Yolanda began, but another bout of coughing stopped her short, and gouts of blood came from her mouth, splattering her clothes and the floor in front of her.

People screamed and backed away, Pamela included. She ended up colliding with the female student she had pushed away, sending the girl back into the power bar display. This time the girl and the entire display toppled to the floor.

Nearby, Jessica screamed, "Get out before you kill us all!" She grabbed up one of the heavy metal travel mugs from the glass display cabinet and tossed it at Yolanda. It hit the cashier in the back of the head.

Pamela wanted to tell Jessica to stop, but she couldn't seem to make herself speak. Or move. She merely stood there watching as others ran to the cabinet and began pelting Yolanda with the travel mugs. Spitting up blood, Yolanda suddenly broke for the door. As soon as she was through, the postal worker closed and locked it again.

"Who else has touched the infected ones?" Baldy shouted with the righteous fury of a televangelist. He pointed at the female student still on the floor among the power bars, the mother and daughter whose husband and father had been caught in the rain, and at Tony.

"Everybody, just listen to me for a minute," Tony

said, but no one got to hear what he had to say. The next thing out of his mouth was a blood-flecked cough.

Eugene held his wife's hand as she dry-swallowed two of the pain pills. They sat in two large chairs by the glass front of the Malerman Center. Helen was still shaky but the pain seemed to be subsiding somewhat, or at least that's what she said.

Eugene glanced out the window, where the sun shone brighter, reflecting off the lake which now had a sheen of translucent sludge on top of it. He would give Helen another moment to rest, and then the two of them were getting in the car and going straight to the hospital. As he gazed out the glass, he saw the door to the bookstore open again. A young girl came rushing out, stumbling and falling to her knees.

"Somebody else just left the store," he said, slowly pushing to his feet.

The young guy who had been pulled in a moment ago ran toward the door. "Is it my girlfriend? Oh no, it's that chick who works behind the counter."

While he watched, Eugene saw the girl retch like she was going to vomit—but all that came out was a crimson drool. *Blood,* he realized. The girl was choking up blood.

3:25pm

Vincent found himself rushing outside for the second time in as many minutes. He was concerned for the girl, of course, but his thoughts were really focused on

Tony. The girl was puking blood, and she'd come from the store. The store where his husband was still shut up. He'd left Tony there, expecting him to be safe.

When Vincent reached the girl, he knelt down near her, careful to avoid the blood that splattered the pavement like a grotesque abstract art project. She continued to retch and gag, and when she looked up at him, he saw that her face had turned an eggplant purple.

Aubergine, he thought randomly.

Her throat seemed puffed up; swollen like the necks of some frogs. Vincent realized that she couldn't breathe. First she'd thrown up blood, and now her throat seemed to be constricting, asphyxiating her.

Vincent wanted to help, but he didn't know what to do. In movies, he'd seen people perform emergency tracheotomies on choking victims with pens, but even if he had a pen, this wasn't a movie and he would have no idea how to do anything like that.

And when he glanced toward the bookstore, he stopped thinking about the girl altogether.

He saw the bald fucker staring back at him through the glass. Then the guy opened his mouth and sprayed blood all over the window before clutching at this throat and collapsing.

Vincent jumped to his feet and ran toward the store.

All around Tony, people were falling to the floor, coughing up blood. He crawled on his hands and knees toward the door. He wheezed, trying to take in great, gulping breaths but managing only the thinnest stream of oxygen. He burned with fever, and his chest ached as if he'd taken a sledgehammer to the sternum.

It seemed to be affecting everyone now, and Tony had no idea what was happening. None of them had been out in the rain.

A pounding made Tony lift his head, which took a surprising amount of energy, and he saw Vincent on the other side of the door, yanking on the handle and banging on the glass. He couldn't get in, of course. They'd locked the doors, thinking they had sealed the sickness outside. Instead, they'd sealed it inside.

He could hear Vincent shouting his name, throwing his body against the door. Plexiglass, not real glass. He wasn't likely to get through. At least not in time to do anything, if anything could be done.

Tony continued to crawl toward the door, but the thin stream of oxygen making it to his aching lungs continued to narrow, and he found all the strength being sapped from his limbs. He collapsed onto his stomach, head titled back so that the last thing he saw would be his husband.

"Daddy, something weird is going on?" Lisa said into the phone as everyone ran back toward the store, banging on the glass. The girl who'd been coughing up blood on the pavement wasn't moving, and Lisa tried to avoid looking directly at her. Unconscious or dead, Lisa wasn't sure she wanted to know.

Her father didn't respond right away, but she could hear him coughing from a distance, as if he were holding the phone away from his mouth.

Halfway between the Malerman Center and the

store, she veered off toward the lake. "Daddy, are you okay? Talk to me?"

He tried to say something, but his words died in another bout of coughing, and his breathing became ragged and labored. She heard a clatter, and then he sounded even more distant. She suspected he'd dropped the phone.

Lisa began running toward the parking lot and her car, all the while screaming "Daddy!" into the phone.

3:26pm

Dena's mother slumped over one of the café tables, the surface of which was slick with blood. She wasn't moving. Dena herself struggled to breathe, her vision beginning to darken around the periphery like ink stains slowly spreading across her field of vision.

At first she thought she was hallucinating her dad, but no—that was him, just outside the window, fists pounding on the glass. He screamed her and her mother's names, but his voice sounded muffled. More muffled than could be explained by the glass. As if Dena's ears had been stuffed with cotton.

She took two staggering steps toward the window, collapsed onto her knees, crawled the rest of the way. She was no longer spitting up blood, but her chin and the front of her shirt were covered in it. At the window, she reached up and placed a palm against the glass. On the other side, her dad did the same. He was crying, and Dena mused that she'd never seen her dad cry before. Not even in the hospital after his heart attack.

She tried to form the words 'I love you, Dad', but

she couldn't seem to make her mouth work. Her hand dropped away, leaving a faint print outlined in red, and then the ink around her vision closed in until there was nothing but blackness.

Eugene led his wife past the people banging at the windows and door of the bookstore. He urged her to look away from the girl lying motionless on the pavement.

"Gene," Helen said, "shouldn't we try to help those people?"

He glanced back at the body on the pavement. He wanted to keep thinking of it as a girl, but he realized that at this point it was just a body.

"We can't help them," he said, still hustling Helen toward the parking lot. "We need to help ourselves now."

Vincent ran to the metal tables in the courtyard outside the bookstore, intending to take one of the chairs and use it to smash through the glass. The boy he'd dragged in out of the rain seemed to have the same idea, and had come with him.

However, they were both thwarted as they discovered the chairs were attached to the tables themselves, and the tables were sunk into the concrete.

Tilting his head back, Vincent howled his frustration at a sky that was now a perfect, unblemished, crystalline blue.

Pamela huddled with her back against the café counter, body quaking with chills, wearing a bib of her own blood. Her chest burned with fire, and her limbs felt too heavy to lift. She tried to get air down her windpipe but to no avail.

As she sensed her consciousness slipping, she moved her eyes around the café, seeing everyone else completely still. Including Baldy: no longer in charge of anything.

She'd allowed her own fear to cloud her better judgment; they all had. They had turned out those who had been exposed to the rain. The very ones outside the store, now pounding on the glass. They seemed lively and healthy enough. Ironic, in a poetic justice sort of way.

Was this a punishment, because they had failed some cosmic test? They'd had the choice between caring for those who they thought might have been infected with something or turning their backs on those people. They had chosen wrong.

Pamela's last coherent thought was, *We're getting what we deserve.*

Excerpt from *The Day the Rains Came: An Annotated Timeline of the Deluge*

THE RAINS STOPPED at 3:23:15pm EST. By 3:40pm EST, 3.2 billion people were dead. The virus hit suddenly, having an incubation period of only moments before causing severe oral hemorrhaging, extreme fever, rapid fluid build-up in the lungs, and angioedema (or swelling) of the trachea that effectively cut off a person's air supply.

Even now, years later, no one has been able to determine the origin of this contagion, its exact mechanisms, or even how it was disseminated. It seems unlikely it could be naturally occurring, considering that it affected people all over the planet at the exact same time. Just as it seems unlikely that the Deluge itself was naturally occurring.

Some have speculated it could have been a biological weapon, a nerve gas of some kind perhaps, but again that begs the question of how it could have been dispersed everywhere at once, not to mention who could have orchestrated such a feat, and to what end?

Inevitably, those on the fringes of science have put forth the hypothesis of extraterrestrial involvement, but as with most hypotheses from these sectors, there is no actual corroborating evidence to support such claims.

What is known now is that the rain itself acted as an inoculant, being absorbed through the skin and triggering an immune response that served to protect from the virus, rendering him or her insusceptible. With all the worry and panic over the rain itself being the vector of a possible sickness, the end result was that those with enough exposure to the rain turned out to be the only ones spared from what could have been an extinction event for the human race.

Which also raises the question: if someone orchestrated the virus, who orchestrated the protective rain that came before it?

As with most questions raised by the Deluge, we may never have answers.

September 24, 20—

VINCENT PULLED HIS car into the lot at 11:43am. Once he'd parked, he sat behind the wheel for another few moments, wondering if this little reunion had been such a good idea. He hadn't been back to the Friedkin campus in six months, not since the day his world had effectively ended.

He and the other Bookstore Survivors, as they had come to call themselves, had kept in touch over social media. He wasn't sure why. In some ways, it was like rubbing salt into a wound: a constant reminder. Then again, everything in the post-Deluge world was a constant reminder. He guessed on some level they needed each other, like a support group or something.

And thus, this little get-together was planned. Some were calling it closure, others a memorial. Vincent wasn't sure what he'd call it, but he felt he needed it just as much as he dreaded it.

Finally he got out of the car and began walking down toward the bookstore. As he did, the door to a green jeep opened and a young man stepped out. Vincent recognized him immediately. Nicholas Mahoney, the young man they'd forced out of the bookstore, the one Vincent had gone out to rescue.

The two men embraced without a word as if they were old friends who had known one another forever.

"How you holding up?" Vincent asked as they started making their way across the lot.

Nick shrugged. "As best as can be expected, I guess. I have to admit, I think about that day a lot, particularly when that guy threw the chair at me and knocked me outside. You know, he probably saved my life."

"That wasn't his intent, that's for sure," Vincent said bitterly.

"Intention doesn't matter, not in the end. I mean, everything I've read suggested the little bit I got on me when I stuck my hand out into the rain probably wouldn't have saved me. If he hadn't knocked me out to get covered in the stuff, really in the nick of time since the rain stopped like a minute later, I'd be as dead as the rest of them now. It kind of hurts my brain to think about it too much."

"Then try not to think about it," Vincent suggested, though he knew that was advice easy to give but near impossible to take. He certainly hadn't been able to heed it himself.

As they neared the bookstore, they saw a couple standing out front, holding hands. Dr. Argentine and Charlie. For a second, Vincent felt the bile of resentment rise, but he pushed it back down. If the two found a little happiness together, good for them. Vincent himself had lost both Tony and Raul, but that wasn't the professor's fault.

Thomas saw Vincent and Nick approaching and he raised his hand in a wave. Any acrimony he'd felt toward Vincent had dropped away. The world was a different place than it had been six months ago, and because of it, everyone's priorities had shifted. Life seemed infinitely more precious, and there simply wasn't room for pettiness.

It won't last, the pragmatist side of Thomas thought. *Given enough time, mankind will once more resort to rancor and trifling grudges.*

Thomas refused to give in to that kind of thinking, however. If the unity the world seemed to be experiencing after such a great tragedy was only temporary, then all the more reason to enjoy it while it lasted.

And Thomas had much to be thankful for—like the young man who held his hand. He smiled at Charlie and Charlie smiled back. Normally being so open about dating a student would have been unthinkable, but Charlie wasn't exactly a student anymore. For that matter, Thomas wasn't exactly a professor. In the wake of everything, Friedkin had yet to reopen for classes, which was the case with most institutions of learning.

The Deluge had changed everything, and it was going to take a while for everyone to adjust and figure out how to move forward.

But Thomas knew he could move forward with Charlie by his side.

Charlie faded into the background as Thomas said hello to the two men, Vincent and Nick. Charlie had always tended toward a natural shyness, but it had been worse since the rain. Since both his parents had died.

He'd stayed here in Greenville, moving in with Thomas. They hadn't really discussed it. Charlie simply had nowhere else to go. It had been convenient.

Just like their relationship. Convenient.

Charlie felt pretty bad about that. He'd turned to Thomas not because of any genuine attraction for the older man, but because he felt like he owed him something for saving his life. Although in retrospect, Charlie had saved Thomas's life as well. Charlie could tell Thomas really cared about him, and Charlie liked Thomas well enough—but honestly, he sort of wished he'd never initiated the sexual component of their relationship.

Oh well, what was done was done. He'd have to deal with the consequences, at least until he figured out what to do next. Thomas provided a safe haven, but their relationship couldn't last.

Eugene arrived at noon on the dot. He walked with a cane, his steps slow and pained. But he was still moving. It would be horribly selfish of him not to be grateful for at least that.

But he wasn't, not really.

He found Vincent, Nick, Thomas, and Charlie sitting at the metal tables in the courtyard between the bookstore and Malerman. The bookstore itself was shuttered and locked, of course, like most of the campus buildings.

"Hey old-timer," Vincent said, offering a handshake.

Eugene said hello to them all and took a seat, happy to be off his feet.

"I was sorry to hear about your wife," Charlie said softly.

Eugene nodded, having to blink back tears before trusting himself to speak. "Thank you. I know you all wanted to come to the funeral, but I thought it best not to have one. Helen was cremated and it seemed fitting not to make too much a fuss about it."

Eugene felt hollow inside, incomplete. He had never thought of his marriage as a co-dependent relationship, but now that Helen was gone, he realized how much he'd defined himself through her. Her absence left such a gaping void in his life that he yearned to surrender to the abyss and be swallowed by it.

The rain had protected Helen from the virus, but it couldn't protect her from the cancer that had been eating her alive. She'd passed only two months after the Deluge.

He'd thought attending this reunion might make him feel better, being surrounded by his fellow survivors. But he discovered he was wrong. He suspected the only thing that would make him feel better would be joining Helen.

Which he hoped wouldn't be too much longer.

Lisa came late. She'd always had a punctuality problem, but these days being on time seemed even less important. She pulled in at nearly 12:25pm.

"Last one to the party," Vincent said as she walked up, with a joviality she could tell he didn't feel.

Lisa scanned the group. “What about Mr. Weathers?”

“Oh yeah,” Vincent said. “Jerry texted me a little while ago. Said he couldn’t make it. He actually got in the car and started driving, but he ended up turning around and going back home.”

Lisa took a seat. “Understandable.”

The man had stood right here and watched his wife and daughter die. Why would he want to come back here? For that matter, why had any of them come back? She’d thought it might help, but looking at the faces surrounding her, she knew that had been a mistake. For all of them.

“How’s your father?” Dr. Argentine asked.

“He’s good,” she said, feeling a little pang at guilt. Almost everyone else here had lost someone close to them, in some cases several someones, but her father had survived.

She had thought she’d lost him for sure, but he hadn’t wanted to tell her when they were talking on the phone that day that he’d run out to the car to get the groceries after the rain started, getting doused. She’d initially thought she was hearing him die over the phone, but he’d simply swallowed some tea down the wrong pipe and been coughing it up. He’d been very lucky.

She’d been very lucky.

It was terrifying just how much luck had been involved here. In parts of the world, the three hours of the rain had come in the middle of the night, meaning almost everyone had been inside and sleeping. Therefore they had succumbed to the virus, all without ever waking. They hadn’t stood a chance.

So yes, survivor's guilt was a real thing to contend with—but Lisa made a silent vow to get past it. She would choose gratitude over guilt.

The reunion lasted barely an hour, everyone claiming other commitments. Vincent understood. He didn't really want to be here anyway.

He stayed the longest, however, telling everyone goodbye and watching them drive away. Then he stood outside the bookstore for a moment, remembering Tony. His goodness, his compassion, his trusting nature.

He'd been too good for Vincent, that was for sure. The question now was: Could Vincent make himself into the kind of man he should have been for Tony?

He didn't know. He really didn't know.

As he walked back across the parking lot, Vincent glanced off across the lake and saw dark storm clouds gathering over the mountains. He got in the car and peeled out as if trying to stay ahead of the rain.

THE END?

Not if you want to dive into more of Crystal Lake Publishing's Tales from the Darkest Depths!

Check out our amazing website and online store.
https://www.crystallakepub.com

We always have great new projects and content on the website to dive into, as well as a newsletter, behind the scenes options, social media platforms, our own dark fiction shared-world series and our very own webstore. If you use the IGotMyCLPBook! coupon code in the store (at the checkout), you'll get a one-time-only 50% discount on your first eBook purchase!

Our webstore even has categories specifically for KU books, non-fiction, anthologies, more books by Mark Allan Gunnells, and of course more novels and novellas.

ABOUT THE AUTHOR

Mark Allan Gunnells loves to tell stories. He has since he was a kid, penning one-page tales that were *Twilight Zone* knockoffs. He likes to think he has gotten a little better since then. He loves reader feedback, and above all he loves telling stories. He lives in Greer, SC, with his husband Craig A. Metcalf.

Readers . . .

Thank you for reading *When It Rains*. We hope you enjoyed this novella.

If you have a moment, please review *When It Rains* at the store where you bought it.

Help other readers by telling them why you enjoyed this book. No need to write an in-depth discussion. Even a single sentence will be greatly appreciated. Reviews go a long way to helping a book sell, and is great for an author's career. It'll also help us to continue publishing quality books. You can also share a photo of yourself holding this book with the hashtag #IGotMyCLPBook!

Thank you again for taking the time to journey with Crystal Lake Publishing.

Visit our Linktree page for a list of our social media platforms. https://linktr.ee/CrystalLakePublishing

Our Mission Statement:

Since its founding in August 2012, Crystal Lake Publishing has quickly become one of the world's leading publishers of Dark Fiction and Horror books in print, eBook, and audio formats.

While we strive to present only the highest quality fiction and entertainment, we also endeavour to support authors along their writing journey. We offer our time and experience in non-fiction projects, as well as author mentoring and services, at competitive prices.

With several Bram Stoker Award wins and many other wins and nominations (including the HWA's Specialty Press Award), Crystal Lake Publishing puts integrity, honor, and respect at the forefront of our publishing operations.

We strive for each book and outreach program we spearhead to not only entertain and touch or comment on issues that affect our readers, but also to strengthen and support the Dark Fiction field and its authors.

Not only do we find and publish authors we believe are destined for greatness, but we strive to work with men and woman who endeavour to be decent human beings who care more for others than themselves, while still being hard working, driven, and passionate artists and storytellers.

Crystal Lake Publishing is and will always be a beacon of what passion and dedication, combined with overwhelming teamwork and respect, can accomplish. We endeavour to know each and every one of our readers, while building personal relationships with our authors, reviewers, bloggers, podcasters, bookstores, and libraries.

We will be as trustworthy, forthright, and transparent as any business can be, while also keeping most of the headaches away from our authors, since it's our job to solve the problems so they can stay in a creative mind. Which of course also means paying our authors.

We do not just publish books, we present to you worlds within your world, doors within your mind, from talented authors who sacrifice so much for a moment of your time.

There are some amazing small presses out there, and through collaboration and open forums we will continue to support other presses in the goal of helping authors and showing the world what quality small presses are capable of accomplishing. No one wins when a small press goes down, so we will always be there to support hardworking, legitimate presses and their authors. We don't see Crystal Lake as the best press out there, but we will always strive to be the best, strive to be the most interactive and grateful, and even blessed press around. No matter what happens over time, we will also take our mission very seriously while appreciating where we are and enjoying the journey.

What do we offer our authors that they can't do for themselves through self-publishing?

We are big supporters of self-publishing (especially hybrid publishing), if done with care, patience, and planning. However, not every author has the time or inclination to do market research, advertise, and set up book launch strategies. Although a lot of authors are successful in doing it all, strong small presses will always be there for the authors who just want to do what they do best: write.

What we offer is experience, industry knowledge, contacts and trust built up over years. And due to our strong brand and trusting fanbase, every Crystal Lake Publishing book comes with weight of respect. In time our fans begin to trust our judgment and will try a new author purely based on our support of said author.

With each launch we strive to fine-tune our approach, learn from our mistakes, and increase our reach. We continue to assure our authors that we're here for them and that we'll carry the weight of the launch and dealing with third parties while they focus on their strengths—be it writing, interviews, blogs, signings, etc.

We also offer several mentoring packages to authors that include knowledge and skills they can use in both traditional and self-publishing endeavours.

We look forward to launching many new careers.

This is what we believe in. What we stand for. This will be our legacy.

Welcome to Crystal Lake Publishing—
Tales from the Darkest Depths.